# CHALLENGER

## Horses Reflect Our Souls

(Horses and Souls Book One)

## Anna Rashbrook

CHALLENGER

Formerly published in 2018 as The Baize Door

# ONE

Tumbleweed! That's all that it would need for complete desolation thought Joanna as she made her way across the showground. The Bank holiday crowds had hit the motorways early to avoid the jams, no fun in this late August heat, so the music from the stalls and marquees had stopped and the quietness was almost a roar. She was still noting things down on her clipboard as she walked along. Despite the extra bin runs, there was still a lot of litter. Bad. But at least this year, now that she had changed the time of the grand parade, the majority of the shiny show jumpers and the now, not overly clean livestock had got away before the masses. Good. She waved to some stall holders who were packing up, but most were taking advantage of the free night's stay on the campsite and would leave tomorrow, just another brilliant idea she'd had.

Joanna broke out in a light sweat as she entered the hospitality tent. The thank-you party for all the stewards, cleaners, cashiers, arena party security and car-park attendants was making an early start. She made her way slowly through all the now familiar faces, thanking and listening and noting any comments or gripes on her overworked board. She took a grip on herself and kept her smile going. Four days of being polite, tactful and sometimes firm would soon be over. She could be as rude as she liked and tell people exactly what she was feeling, but until later this evening, she was the face and buck stopping point of the Hazeley show. So many people had asked her where Ray was, and she'd had to explain so often that he was away, that it had become a pre-programmed response. Some of the older folk had shaken their heads and gone away muttering, but most had accepted and welcomed her.

Finally, she reached the bar and ordered the double G&T she'd promised herself from Thursday night. Draught tonic water. In a pint glass. With ice. No lemon. Perfect. Let her hair down from the tight bun. Loosen the tight jacket. Underneath she was still buzzing but knew that tomorrow she would be so tired that she would slob in bed all morning, dozing until she began to remember all the things that needed doing in the run down and clearing up. At least the team from the estate knew their jobs and their moans would be by phone. Her precious glass was nearly knocked out of her hand as Gloria pounced on her.

'You won't believe what a day we've had, not to mention how many people shopped, dropped and forgot!' she shouted. Another headache for Joanna, what to do with all the forgotten goods. 'But we had a brill idea!'

Joanna looked askance.

'We got everyone to leave a phone number on the slips, here you are!!!' Joanna took the limp envelope and tried to smile. More phone calls.

'Come on you old bat, stop looking like you've been knocked over by a steamroller and drink up! Take that bloody yellow hair of yours down and relax!' She lugged Joanna over to the rest of the Shop and Drop Gang, who she clocked were in their old school uniform, and for the first time in days, she laughed out loud.

'You bunch of tramps! How many of you got propositioned by the Young Farmers?'

'All of us!!!'

'And are you going home like that?'

'You bet, all the kids are having a sleepover at Granny's and Shaun's got the champagne on ice!' They all burst out laughing at Gloria's bad wink.

Joanna suddenly felt so tired she just wanted to cry, not only because she had no Shaun to go home to but also because the house would be dark and empty. She glugged her drink and then out of the corner of her eye she saw a woman, not in uniform standing on the edge of the group, chatting to Marina. She looked familiar, but Joanna couldn't place her. She was looking around her like she was looking for a bolt hole too. With an ally, Joanna could go, she sidled over. 'Um, I'm sorry, I don't remember your name, but you look like you could do with a lift to the car park?'

'That would be kind, my car's at the far end,' the woman smiled gently. Dammit, who was she? 'Come on then, follow me.'

Under the roar of laughter at one of Gloria's jokes, Joanna pulled at one of the tent flaps with years of expertise at escaping and they were quickly outside in the semi-fresh air. 'I stowed my wheels here earlier for such an escape!'

The golf buggy was just around the corner of the tent. They bundled in and took off quite speedily. Joanna didn't want to go home on her own. 'Don't suppose you fancy a drink and something back at my place?' She turned to the stranger, and the light caught her face at a new angle. 'Oh heavens, it's you isn't it, Diane where have you been all this time?' At which point the buggy ground to a halt, its battery given out after hours of hard work. 'Rats,' was the best Joanna could manage. And she sat blindly at the wheel, the stress of the past few days topped with this was too much.

Diane laid a gentle hand on her arm. 'I'm a bit of a shock aren't I!! Yes, let's go to the house, we can talk on the patio like we used to,' she said in a fake cheerful voice.

Joanna, for once in her life not full of words nodded. They sat for a moment, looking each other up and down. To Joanna, Diane looked just the same, dark brown hair and big eyes, only with make-up and older.

'You did get your ears pierced then!' Diane broke the pause.

'I won Dad over after a struggle! But just look at us, we're both the same height and you used to tower over me!'

'No more ponies for us any more.'

Joanna grimaced,' I don't ride at all, it's a long story! But you're so much thinner, you used to call me skinny! Now I'm the plump one!'

'But you're not! We're women, not kids any more. Oh, how do we see ourselves?' Diane linked her arm through Joanna's and they made their way up the lane to the house, both now silent not knowing where to take it further. They reached the main gate where the Victorian house stood silhouetted in the evening sun. Built in red brick with tall windows edged with green shutters, it sat regally in the heat. With no cars parked for once on the old carriage round, it seemed like time had stood still.

'I'm sorry, I can't let you come any further, the house is off bounds to the public.' In front of them stood a security guard in an ill-fitting uniform with long ginger hair sticking out from under the cap.

'I'm Joanna Hazeley, and this is my guest.'

'I need to ask for some form of identification.'

Joanna looked down and found to her dismay that her ID card was long gone. 'Look, Mr Security. Man. I am who I say I am, there is the main house, and I can show you where the front door key is, I'll let you in and give you proof."

'I'm sorry I can't do that. Now please leave the premises.'

'This is ridiculous! I haven't seen a single guard here all week, what's the problem now?'

'I'm just doing extra cover for the permanent staff while they go to a party,' he said, wiping sweat and hair across his forehead. The penny dropped with Joanna, all the staff were at the party she had so cleverly organised...she pulled her mobile out of her pocket. The guard stood glaring at them, arms now folded, foot tapping, waiting for the next move.

'Hi, Stan...Yes, I love you too.' The party was obviously doing very well without her. 'Look, I've got a real jobs-worth security guard here, who I guess is one of yours, and he's not letting me in the house, what the dickens is going on?' Joanna handed the phone over, and there came a flow of what was clearly unpleasant, and the guard blushed.

'My apologies.' He returned the phone and with a stiff back walked away. Joanna turned to Diane, 'I'd forgotten Dad muttering something about keeping an eye on the place. It was after the arena party had an impromptu pool party last year that we realised we needed to look at security. I guess I wasn't briefed properly; apparently, there's been guards here all week! Come on, let's get that drink!'

Under the portico, Joanna fumbled for the keys and opened the bright yellow door. Inside, the little hall was cool and quiet, the red and black tiles glowing in the evening sun. 'We've had a few things done since you were last here, we've got central heating and a pool in the footings of the old east wing,' Joanna wittered, not knowing what to say, so great was the enormity of this meeting.

She kicked off her hard-worked shoes, and they went through the dining room into the kitchen. 'Coke, lemonade or another gin?' she proffered. It seemed Diane was also now getting nervous as she smiled weakly and helped herself to the coke.

'Do you remember the old furnace in the cellar? When it was taken out last year, we had a huge surprise as we found a blocked off door, and behind it, we discovered all the family documents, deeds, maps, oh, it's astonishing! It seems that the accounts of the visits Nelson and Mrs Hamilton made will cause huge interest. We thought all had been lost in the fire. Come and have a look, we used some of the show money to put in a controlled climate room, so we can store everything. I've been cataloguing it with help from the local Record office, it's so fascinating.' Joanna knew she was babbling again as she went out of the kitchen and turned left to the cellar door. 'We've got it all sorted, no more frightening oil boiler. New stairs and everything. Just be careful, the door handle on the inside came off the other day and we couldn't find it, we've got a piece of string holding it open, there's another door at the foot of the steps.'

So of course, Diane's handbag caught the handle as she passed down, the door slammed.

'Oh no, I'm so sorry, what have I done?'

The pair stood and looked at each other frozen. Joanna pulled herself together.

'Come downstairs, we might be trapped and not have a mobile signal, but in the office is a PC with a good old-fashioned landline, we'll reach someone.' When they went through the door, Joanna turned the air con up a bit, it felt cold after the summer evening. She switched the PC on. In silence, they watched as it wouldn't connect.

'I think we'll be here until Dad gets back later tonight. We can hear footsteps when he arrives, the main entrance is above us. Oh no, did you have to be somewhere?'

'No, not at all. And maybe this is a Godsend Joanna, I came here to talk to you, we, you, I have so much to tell you. Will, you let me talk the whole thing through, then tell me what your feelings are?'

Joanna nodded, and settled to listen, trying to keep her mind open and not let her own memories and feelings cloud her judgement. She looked at her friend and saw the thin teenager with the scraped back hair and tatty jodhpurs still within the older woman. Heard Take That, blazing out in the stable yard as they groomed horses in the sunshine and their giggling about stupid things as they rode down the lanes. It might only have been a year of friendship, but it had been intense as they had lived in each other's pockets, sharing secrets and frustrations. It seemed they had buddied up for life, and then it had been so brutally broken.

'I found our friendship and the horses one of the best things that ever happened to me,' Diane echoed Joanna's thoughts. 'The show jumping, the hacking and mucking about. I know some said that it was odd with our age difference we shouldn't be knocking about together, but I didn't care. 17 and 12 was a big gap on paper, but you were my first real mate. We'd moved around so much with Dad's job. Here was the longest we've ever stayed put, and it was good.'

'Wasn't that show, just somehow perfect? Weather, ground, horses going so well? The sun shone just like today and on that last day, everything seemed to come together in the ring. Shadow was just one with me and I've never jumped such a good clear round since. We had the strides between the triple perfect and she flew over the water jump like a star. We even cut the corner by the oxer without a hitch.'

'I was just so on a high when I came out of the ring that I couldn't believe it when I saw the men stood with Mum. She'd been arguing with them to give me enough time to jump before we were marched away. In some ways, it was a good thing having Shadow with us, as we had to take her. If she'd been at home, they'd have just…well, I don't even want to think of it. As it was, we had to bundle everything into another trailer and two highly armed men drove us all the way to Northumberland. As we left the grounds, I heard over the loudspeaker I'd won but of course, couldn't collect the cup.'

'The safe house was in a small valley completely surrounded by woods, but maybe easy to guard. It had stables and so in a way, at least I could ride, or so I thought. That night Mum and I were briefed, or as I'd rather like to think, lied to. They never told us in so many words whether Dad was already dead or was being held hostage; where he was or what was happening. They held us in limbo for almost a week. Mum and I kept the routine of not talking about things, trying to be positive. She took to more praying and being quiet and trying to tell the men about her faith as she did last time it happened. All I could do was muck out and groom. I wasn't allowed to ride anywhere.'

'Then came the big black car, and we knew the worst had happened. Dad had left orders that we were not to be told exactly what had happened, so we didn't have nightmares imagining, but I'm not sure that was better than not knowing at all. The MOD is master of withholding and giving misinformation. We never knew any more than he had left us, and we couldn't even bury him. We had to grieve for a phantom. They did lighten up after this, I expect they needed the men somewhere else. Whatever the risk was before, I guess we weren't such a high priority.

After a couple of weeks, Mum mutinied. She threw them out, and we had to once again go house hunting. We couldn't come back here because of the security risk, whatever that was if it ever existed. And we didn't want to stay in Northumberland. So, we went back to her home village in Wales. I did write, but I dare say they never reached you and I gave up after a while.'

'I finished my A levels, and with a new name and identity, I got into show jumping. They even tried to get me to wear a wig at first, it was just ridiculous. It took us years to shake officialdom off. We had a shed load of money from Dad's estate and I had some brilliant horses. I always wondered if our paths would cross and as the fuss had died down; we could get in contact again. Then, all sorts of things happened. I took a course in equine-assisted therapy, it helped me with some issues, and I want to make a business of it. The yard where I have my business needs me to move the horses, so they can do other stuff. Wales is not only too remote but there are already other people in the same field. Whatever happened to Dad, the risk is long gone, because we're finally going to have a monument for him in the local church – you know he was born here? Mum and I have rented a place in Hampton while I look about. But I do so need to touch base with you, explain things... I've never made great friends, and maybe I'm looking back with rosy tinted spectacles. I know it was a long time ago now, and maybe it's too late. What do you think?'

Joanna was staring at the wall taking it all in and tussling with her emotions. She could just agree and let Diane go on thinking she had won and have to live with a half-truth, but it was such a pivotal movement in her own life that she also needed to tell the truth. She couldn't live with secrets, and if they were starting on a clean slate, it had to be said. She took a deep breath.

'I think you need to hear me out too. That day changed me as well. I've never told anyone this, not even Dad. I rode into that collecting ring with Mum's voice behind me, you've warmed him up, don't let him relax, don't slump like a sack of potatoes, watch what they're all doing and do better. Cut their times, see how you can beat them. The County cup will be yours. You're a winner and so on. Even after three years, she was still with me.'

'I saw your perfect round and saw it as a threat. I had wanted to win the cup for so many years for myself and under Mum's pressure. I wasn't going to let anyone be better than me. I could top what you did. I wanted that cup on the sitting room mantelpiece. I didn't care about the gossip that I shouldn't be allowed to enter, that I had an unfair advantage in knowing the land. I rode in more determined than I had ever been than when Mum was alive. That bell rang, and I saw how I could cut your time if I cut the corner by the oxer harder than you, I was determined to beat you. It wasn't a beautiful round, I pushed Challenger as I'd never done before, and he gave me his best, even if I didn't respect that at the moment. And I did it, I cut your time by half a second.'

As I rode out of the ring, Challenger was soaked in sweat and I knew he'd pulled that tendon again. I was so ashamed. Winning had been more important than respecting that bloody good round you'd ridden and allowing you the honour. I'd thrashed my horse. All for something that would be gossiped about in the village; there would be no respect or accolade. All I'd thought about was winning. I even threw up outside the ring. And I vowed I would never be what Mum wanted, a pot hunting winner. I wasn't going to make up for all her failures and disappointments any more. She was gone and couldn't hold me any more. No more living her life for her. No more. I was done with horses.

I led Challenger to the Secretaries tent and withdrew, but not without a lot of arguing. I left them sorting out the mess. That was the announcement you heard. I tried to find you, but your box had disappeared. I thought you'd left because of what I'd done. I felt it was all I could do, and it was the right thing.

Then I walked Challenger slowly home. In the evening, I sat down and told Dad I was giving up the horses, I told him I didn't want to live out Mum's dreams for her, she had lost that right by dying. He found it so difficult to understand because I didn't tell him the bit about beating you. I let him think I had withdrawn due to Challenger's injury. He argued, saying how I could just hack about and have fun. But it was all or nothing for me.

Finally, he said he would deal with it all. Which meant that the next day Challenger disappeared in a horse box and the stables were closed. I didn't go near them for years. I tried to visit you, but the house was empty, not a sign you'd ever lived there. I never got your letters, maybe the MOD thought I was a threat. Now I know why you disappeared, I'm selfishly glad you didn't go because of me. I was so self-centred that I never thought it was something to do with your dad, even though you had hinted at things.'

They both sat in silence for a minute. 'Diane, I'd still value your friendship, do we need forgiveness or just pick up where we left off, but without the horses for me?'

Diane paused and then spoke slowly. 'We must start afresh, you short, fat, batch for thrashing me anyway!' she tried to laugh. 'Water under the bridge and all that stuff. It doesn't matter today. You were always set on beating me, but it never bothered me, I never had your manic competitive streak, I liked the winning, but it was the horses and the fun I enjoyed more.'

'So, it was that apparent?'

'Oh yes, and I'm so glad I never met your Mum, I think she would have terrified me!'

They were both a bit sniffly, and it was with relief that they heard footsteps across the ceiling. Joanna leapt up and ran up the stairs,

'Dad, Dad, the flipping door's gone again, let us out!'

The door opened, and Ray stood at the top of the stairs. 'I thought I told you to sort this weeks ago.' Then his gaze went over Joanna's shoulder and he went very pale.

'Good grief, Diane, what the dickens happened to you and what are you doing here now?'

# TWO

'Now just how am I supposed to let the contractors in, with the stables still full of bloody horses?' In waking, Joanna had unconsciously answered her phone, Stan's loud voice would raise the dead.

'Just how many, Stan?'

'Well maybe it's just two, the box has broken down.'

'Tell them to bring the horses up here and either put them in an empty box or the paddock until it's sorted.' Stan grunted and rang off. At least he thought she was still in charge! Joanna slumped back in bed, her head pounding with a headache from the champagne her father had produced to celebrate what he called the return of the native. It had been a relief to let Diane tell her story again, and then just get on to catching up and hearing of her plans for the therapy. Happily, he hadn't passed comment about the real reason for Joanna's giving up riding.

It hadn't gone on late into the evening, but after the stress of the show, Joanna had been nodding on the sofa. Ray had insisted he take Diane back to her car, so Joanna had crashed. Now she was glad to have some space to gather her thoughts for a few minutes before she had to go down with Ray to the showground to see how things were going.

She sat up in bed and tried to think. But all that she felt was a sense of relief and pleasure that Diane had returned, and all had been sorted out. It would be good if she had a mate again; most of her friends had either moved away or were being mumsy. She shied away from all that, it was something not visible on her horizon. Even Gloria had kids. They had all gone in so many different ways and the clique of friends who had sworn eternal friendship had dwindled over the years.

Maybe if she had gone to University after Six form college, things might have been different. Yet she couldn't in her mind's eye see any other alternative. What would have happened if Diane hadn't disappeared? Would they now be the top show jumpers in the country or competing at the Olympics? She shook her head in dismay. No, things were better as they were.

The gradual progression of the little she had done to help with the show had sort of grown over the years into her present role. She liked it, the making it bigger and better over the years; working hard with Dad so it was now a national event.

A few years ago, she would have been now down with Stan starting to organise the clearing of the site; taking the stables and arenas down. Now, contractors and the estate team dealt with that. Joanna was relieved not to have that hard grind any more, despite what fun it had been. She liked her wages and her little flat. Life had worked out okay. Did she want all this to change with Diane's arrival? She was sure this was only the beginning of something.

She got out of bed and stretched. Too much inner absorption wasn't good. She looked out of her window onto the cobbled stable yard at the back of the house. Funny, it was if she hadn't seen it for years. The two horses were being turned out in the paddock, and an idea formed. So obvious that she wondered with a tint of malice if this had been Diane's ulterior motive in the first place. Then she remembered that she had left the air-con on in the cellar and it must be altered. Even if the documents had survived in a hot room behind the boiler for years, they were fragile. Her tiredness dissipated with the need to get on with work.

Afterwards, she made her way through to the dining room where Ray was sitting with a pile of mail and a large jug of coffee.

'Caffeine?' Joanna gratefully took the cup and slumped on a chair.

'So, how was the running of it then, I had to resist not ringing you up!'

'Oh, Dad, it was fun, stressful, hard work and I must admit, I was glad when it was over! Some of the older farmers wouldn't let me help with their problems. I had to get Stan to talk to them. But it did seem that the majority of the livestock were away before the crowds. Oh, and I've got a bone to pick with you. You might have mentioned that you had told Stan to hire guards to keep an eye on the place. A real jobs-worth accosted me. He wouldn't let us in until I rang him last night!'

'Sorry, I meant to say something. We'll get feedback over the next few days from the staff and see how you did.'

Joanna had been expecting some form of congratulation for a good job, but before she could let herself into a bit of self-pity he continued and deflected her thoughts.

'But most importantly, are you truly okay with Diane surfacing like that?'

'It took me right back to being on Challenger again and all my memories of that time. But I don't regret it. But I've just had a devious idea. She wants to open a small riding school, doing riding and horse therapy and stuff. Maybe she has come back to test the ground and see if she can use our stables. She always used to admire them. But maybe she could rent it, it's not been used for years and I guess all that would need doing is the arena re-surfacing.'

Ray looked at her doubtfully over his glasses, 'I thought you'd walked away from that?'

'I wouldn't have anything to do with it,' she replied indignantly. 'I was just trying to be helpful, and I'm interested to see if she has come with this agenda. We were both manipulative. Do you remember my one and only Halloween party?'

Ray grimaced.

'And it would be nice to see if we are still friends after all.'

'Well, it could be nice to have some nags around the place, reminds me of Mia, despite all her failings as a mother.'

'Oh crumbs, am I being selfish; would that rake it all up again?'

'Not at all, I think I've come to terms with all that. Water under the bridge etc etc.'

'Did you know what her dad did? At the time, no one spoke about it, especially to us kids.'

'All I know is that he was something very high up in special forces and might have had things to do with hostages. Apart from that Chloe kept stum.'

'It'll be nice to see her again, won't it? She was always great with sympathy and sandwiches at the shows.'

'Um, maybe better than your mother!' They grinned at each other, but as usual, didn't go any deeper into talking about her. After her death it had been easier just to comfort each other but not go into any personal discussion. They avoided it yet again.

'So, you would be OK with it?'

'Think about it for a few days. We'd have strangers about, we will also have to sort parking, but shall we have a look around this evening? Now, we must go down to the grounds and see how it's all going. Did I tell you we've got to find a new sponsor for the county cup, Alliots have pulled out?' They both rose and went to face the day, putting the show to bed as they had been doing for years.

The stable yard was cool in the evening shade, and as Joanna pulled the door open into the main block.

Despite the years of emptiness, she caught a breeze of hay, horse and leather. She saw her ponies again and felt a sudden pang of pain. Had she made the right decision in walking away? The looseboxes were clean and would only need the automatic drinkers re-attaching. Through into the tack room, the empty racks, hooks and cupboards became a rebuke. How could she have just thrown all this away? The tack and equipment must have cost thousands; let alone the feed, and even the horses themselves. How had Dad got rid of it all and she never noticed? She must have had her head so firmly in the sand! Was it all teenage emotion?

She walked out and opened the small door to what used to be the carriage house, but now had two further looseboxes in it. All clean, as if that part of her childhood had been swept away forever. Did she want all this back again and not be part of it? She wandered back out into the heat and saw the two horses feasting in the paddock. They would be collected that evening. But just the swish of their tails and the munching took her back to being twelve again. She closed her eyes.

'Is it all coming back? Can you bear it? You're so like your mother, it was all or nothing for her too.' Ray put his arm around her shoulders. 'I did say wait a while, but like Mia, instant decisions!'

'I think I must at least try it Dad for Diane's sake. Maybe it will all come back, and you'll be broke again!'

'Not likely, you can pay for it yourself now… Joanna, there's someone here to see you.' She looked into the sun.

'CHLOE!' Looking pretty much as she remembered her, Diane's mum was grinning from ear to ear with the same long blonde hair and wearing her trademark long, flowing skirt. For the first time in many years, Joanna without reservation threw herself into someone's arms.

'You don't know how good it is to see you!' They looked at each other, both welling up.

'Joanna a woman! I still see you as my proxy daughter!' Joanna stiffened; she never wanted a second mother, one was enough.

Chloe went on unabated. 'Oh my, I hope the years have blessed you, little one!' she smiled. 'I should have tried harder to contact you, but things were…well difficult.'

'Don't worry, from what Diane says we all bolted in one way or another. Are you okay?' Joanna looked into the deep blues eyes and felt a peace she hadn't for years. Then she shied away again like a startled horse. 'Where's Diane?'

'Looking at the surface of the outdoor school, probably having a canter on a 20 metre circle!' The laughter was of relief as they all turned and walked to the school. And Diane really was pacing around like a dressage horse and turned bright red at being caught.

'I must admit to having coveted your yard, I used to dream of having my horse at home like you and even looking out of my bedroom window at the horses when I woke up. I was jealous!'

'Well, you still ain't getting the bedroom. I sleep in that side of the house now! So, was this all a ruse to get your hands on my stables????'

Diane had the grace to go redder and look at the ground.

'Well, I did sort of hope to bump into you, before I plucked up the courage to knock on your door!'

'Devious bitch!' glared Joanna in mock anger and they all laughed. Ice broken, the four looked around the stables. Diane went off into great detail as ideas came to her. Joanna found herself completely uninterested which surprised her; but just put it down to it not being her thing any more. It was all for Diane. She would have no part, no, she would look out of her window and gaze at the horses. She wouldn't lift a fork, haynet or saddle.

# THREE

It seemed to Joanna that the next few weeks passed in a blur of renewed friendship, new boundaries, and new noises, re-fitting what she now saw as a very quiet life. Before the horses arrived, Diane had feed, hay and wood shavings delivered. The outdoor school had a new surface put down, a small area was flattened for a lorry and car park. All the fences were checked and repaired so there was constant noise and busyness. Diane was constantly in the house with questions and ideas; it was both wearing and endearing.

On the day the horses were due to arrive Joanna wandered over to the stables with some coffees. She found Diane cleaning the windows in the tack room. They sat down and looked around.

'I just can't wait! They've been out at grass while I've been sorting myself out. It'll be grand. Oh, do you know if our old blacksmith is still around?'

Joanna shook her head, 'No idea, but why don't you look in the phonebook!!! I've lost all my contacts.'

'I have another question, one that you may not like...I've been thinking about the logistics of running this place and the to-ing and froing from Mum's. You've made it quite clear you're not going to to get involved, so I was wondering if I could use the rooms above as a flat...' Diane slurped her coffee and waited for an answer.

'I hadn't thought about that, but you must check with Dad. I guess he won't mind. But I don't think there's any electricity up there, let's look.' Joanna led the way up the stairs feeling both manipulated and sort of happy. The narrow stairs led to the two rooms above the stables, which had earlier been haylofts. No kitchen, just an old wood burner, but thankfully electric points.

'No water though. I suppose it could be linked to the tack room supply,' Diane pointed out. She was bouncing around, wiping the grubby windows and testing the boards which covered the old hay shutes into the boxes.

'But it was lived in in the past. The photo in my living room shows curtains up her. They must have lived so frugally! I suppose it was warm with the heat from the horses, but there's no insulation and we're right under the roof.'

'No problem, I've still got lots of my inheritance to blow. It wouldn't cost much....' Diane was glowing with excitement, but Joanna was having misgivings. Did she want Diane right on her doorstep all the time? She valued her privacy; would she feel overlooked? Everything seemed to be snowballing out of control; becoming like an invasion. 'As I said, you must talk to Dad first. But I guess it may be OK. You must realise this is a big change for him.' Oooh, clever buck passing there thought Joanna to herself.

'I'm sure he won't mind! We could put a kitchen diner sitting room in this room that the stairs go into and then an en-suite into the back room.'

'You won't be able to see the horses from your bedroom though!'

'Never mind, but I'd be with them! And another thing, can you and Ray help me with the website and book-keeping?'

Would it never end? The woman was more a steamroller than a snowball. It hadn't been so bad when it was all the horsey things, not so much on Joanna's doorstep. Then Joanna's humour broke through. What the heck, she had been so lonely last winter. Even if it was with flipping horses, there'd be some life around and fertiliser for the garden. She was smiling as Chloe joined them, the excitement was infectious even if she wouldn't have any part in it.

'You know, I thought last night I ought to have a sign near the main road.' Diane was looking down the drive to the main road.

Joanna turned and looked at her thoughtfully and then grinned.

'Elm Tree Riding School!' They both roared with laughter remembering one of their favourite pony books, which they'd both enjoyed despite their age difference. 'You know, I've still got all my books, couldn't part with them!' Laughed Joanna and they smiled for maybe the first time in their old camaraderie.

At that exact moment, just like in best pony stories, the transporter grumbled into the yard. The four horses were quickly unloaded and turned out into the home paddock. There was the expected careering around as they tested the boundaries and then their heads went down as they saw the surfeit of grass. Four hairy-footed, broad-backed greedy cobs, bay, grey and palomino.

'Maybe we should have taken the top off the field,' remarked Ray joining them. 'None of them are showing their ribs.'

'Let them pig out for a bit Ray, they'll soon eat that off, it's not new grass,' replied Diane. Joanna jumped, she rarely called Dad by his Christian name although she thought it. Somehow, she had expected Diane to too, it felt odd, but what else would she call him? She had always called Chloe by her name. What had Diane called Dad before? Mr H?

Her musing ended as Diane called them over to unload tack and all the gear that follows horses around. Soon the tack room took on the smell and cosiness of a used room. Into they unloaded into the school, poles, a big inflated ball, cones and bits of jumps. It looked like a horsey jumble sale. What was Diane doing with all this junk? Job finished, they stood and leant on the fence again and watched the horses stuffing their faces.

'How do you fancy coming out for a hack with me? The horses have been turned out for a couple of months and I could do with some help getting them fit.'

'No. I don't want to ride anymore, I think I'm happier just looking from a distance.'

'I don't see what harm going for a plod on one of these would do, they're all bone idle. The rides here are so beautiful. No traffic; we could just potter and natter.'

'Diane, I just don't want to. I closed the door on all this. I'm not going to have my life run by horses. I'm happy with my work on the show, and it's a good place.'

'It's only a bleeding hack.'

'Look no. I'm ready to help with your books and things, but, no. We should go down to the Pub together one night, or into Southampton to the clubs…'

'Maybe we could, once I've got the flat sorted.'

Joanna saw Chloe looking quizzically at them but avoided making eye contact and turned back to gaze at the horses. Maybe it had been a huge mistake, they should have just made up and left it at that. No trying to rekindle a friendship that was long dead. She didn't want all this brought up again after all.

# FOUR

'I can't believe how swiftly you've done all this; it looks amazing!' Joanna was leaning over Ray's shoulder looking at the computer screen.

'It was what I was doing when you were running the show. I felt we must keep up with IT and use it to up our marketing. I'm thinking of putting it on Twitter and making a Facebook page. What do you think?'

Joanna felt somewhat ashamed that she had never asked him what he'd been up to when he was away. 'I think that's brilliant, you're more in touch than I am. I only remember Facebook every now and then! How very un-with it I am!'

A very funky website was on the screen advertising Hazeley Stables as the latest thing in riding for kids in the area and the best place to try the new healing therapy. In a slideshow, the clients seemed to be playing odd games with the horses; putting halters on upside down, taking the horses for walks, having group hugs, doing anything but riding.

'This therapy looks most odd, but I guess I'm out of touch with the way the horse world has changed', she mused feeling old. 'Seeing the place in a photo and in these films makes it seem like somewhere else; a high-end professional place. Not just a thing Diane has done!'

'Well, she has done a lot to the place, maybe as we're with it all the time we haven't taken on the changes. Did you know that she's done a whole load of training for this, and she works with a therapist in Southampton?"

'Oh right, no I didn't. Even so, all this hippy get in touch with your inner self-thing isn't my cup of tea at all.' Joanna was taken aback at Ray's slightly defensive tone, so she changed the subject. 'How did you get on with finishing that Ikea flat pack bedroom for her?'

'Um, I got Stan and the lads to do it, I was just breaking bits off!'

'We're neither of us good at DIY!' Joanna sniggered.

'Anyway, just what do you think is your stuff then?' Ray didn't seem to want to be diverted from the subject. Joanna thought for a moment.

'Helping you run the show. Looking after the documents; just enjoying life I suppose.'

'That doesn't seem a lot for someone in their twenties. When did you last go out with Jim?'

'Back off Dad, that's not parent territory.' Joanna couldn't help noticing her voice rising as she lied. 'He's out in the USA on a business trip…What's happened about the County trophy, have any of the customers responded to the letter?'

Ray sighed but went with the rapid change of subject. 'No one as yet, but we have the mince pie party month coming up and the Christmas bash so I guess we'll plug it then. There's still time.'

'How about a montage of all the previous sponsors in the next newsletter? I could ring round and get some comments on how raising the profile helped their business?'

'I'm not so sure that's a good idea. I think most do it as a tax dodge and an easy way to do customer hospitality without having to organise too much.'

'So why not market it as so?'

'Now maybe, that's an idea! But we must be careful over the tax dodge wording! Now can you find me that old picture of the stables, I want to use it for a silhouette in the banner.'

Joanna glanced out of the window as she was taking the picture down off the wall and saw a sleek car parked in the yard. A woman got out and began to encourage the other occupant in the back. After a while, a hunched-up teenager got out and listlessly followed her to the school. Intrigued, Joanna went up to her bedroom and watched. Two of the horses were loose in the school, where Diane was waiting for her customers. All three stood there for a while then the kid was offered some rope and given some instructions. There was a lot of gesticulating from the lad but eventually, he sloped off, and the other two retreated to a corner. The horses sensed his approach and slowly marched away from him, just fast enough that he didn't reach them. Soon they were in the corner of the school, and they reacted by swiftly turning heel and trotting away. He mooched after them again, body hunched over. Joanna could see him mouthing something and was glad she couldn't hear. It all had the same effect, the horses took themselves away. After three or four times, the therapist said something to him. The result appeared to be a hissy fit, and the rope was slung at the horses, who took no notice of him now that he was out of range. He picked up the rope and approached at a different speed, even Joanna could see his anger. He was going to get flattened or kicked, what the hell was Diane playing at? Did she have insurance?

She watched, holding her breath. To her surprise, the horses stopped at his more forceful approach and looked at him. He went to the first, threw the rope around its neck and with all his force pulled the horse back towards the gate.

After one tug, the horse followed obediently. The lad stopped in surprise. So did the horse. He pulled. The horse followed all the way back. As he succeeded, the lad began to straighten up. In a few yards, he'd changed. When he got to the gate, there was almost a grin on his face. A lot of conversation ensued, but Joanna could see the lad surreptitiously stroking the horse on the further side. He continued to be brighter, and he led the horse around the arena looking far more cheerful.

As the session seemed to come to an end, he walked back to the car almost a different kid. What on earth was going on wondered Joanna? She'd never seen horses acting or being used like that before. Perhaps she would take some coffee and cake over to Diane later on…or maybe she would watch a little more. She was intrigued. Joanna had always enjoyed the contact with horses, the grooming and just doing stuff with them. She remembered when she played with her ponies; not to mention the time she had painted her grey shetland with her paints. Mia had been furious, but the pony hadn't minded. It had all come off with the hosepipe.

Maybe it wasn't so wrong just to do stuff with horses, not just riding and competing all the time. Whatever, she wasn't going back there, watching from the window was enough! Remembering the picture, Joanna guiltily went back downstairs. But Ray had disappeared, the computer switched off. She left the picture there and went to find him.

She found him talking to Diane and Chloe in the car park. He turned and had a big grin on his face. What on earth was going on?

'Oh, good, glad you found us. There's a new arrival coming to the stables and I think you might be interested.'

'What sort of arrival?'

'You'll see.'

'Diane, you tell me, I hate surprises.'

'Nope, you'll know soon enough!'

'Chloe??'

Even Chloe just grinned at her. Before Joanna could get the thumbscrews out, and as if on cue; a landrover and trailer pulled into the yard. The driver was familiar, but Joanna couldn't quite place him. He jumped out and with Diane's help opened the trailer and put the ramp down. As they did, Joanna realised it was security man, but this time he didn't seem to be so cross and his hair was pulled back in a ponytail. In fact, he said very little as Diane slowly backed a large dark bay horse down the ramp. Joanna suddenly became aware that everyone, even security man, were looking expectantly at her.

'What? It's just a horse.' Joanna was even more confused.

'Look carefully.'

She did, and something like a sense of shame and fear started to creep across her as she took in the three white socks, the small white snip under the forelock, and the scar down its shoulder.

'OMG, it's Challenger! Where did you find him? Why is he here?'

'Well, I never sold him,' said Ray. 'He's been on loan to a small yard near Bournemouth. He's taught many kids to ride, and now he's retired. I thought it is time to bring him home.'

'Right, Diane, you're going to use him for your therapy thingy?' Joanna didn't want or dare to ask if he had ever recovered from his torn tendon, which had been her fault. She felt so guilty, that even now, she didn't want the answer.

'Actually, that's up to you. He's still your horse.' Joanna was aware she must look like a goldfish, and everyone seemed to be waiting on her.

Security man took action in the awkward pause, Joanna just had time to realise he had pale green eyes and that was quite something before he handed Joanna the rope.

'Well, here he is, I guess he's all yours, and now I must be off.' He nearly smiled. His action broke the impasse, and the others went to help put the ramp back up and take a few things out of the trailer. Joanna looked at the horse and said his name softly. His head swung around with ears pricked. He sniffed her hand, and with a start, pulled back to the end of the rope.

As soon as Joanna tried to get closer he swung back again, his ears now flattened against his head. She tried saying his name soothingly, but that produced a lunge that was going to bite. He stepped back and reared; his hooves narrowly missing Joanna.

'Diane! There's something the matter, come here, I think he's gone mad,' screamed Joanna.

The others turned from talking to security man and saw Challenger pulling away again into another rear. Diane came over, took the rope from Joanna and began soothing him. He calmed down immediately as Joanna backed away.

'Maybe you've got some perfume on he doesn't like, or he didn't like your body language. Look he's fine now, come and stroke him again.'

Now completely nervous, Joanna approached very carefully, but Challenger straight away put his ears back and bared his teeth again in no uncertain terms.

'You can keep him he's clearly had bad treatment or is ill; psychotic even. He's all yours. I never wanted him back in the first place. I don't know what you were thinking Dad. How many times have I told you I'm through with horses?! Just what do you expect me to do?'

Joanna stormed off ignoring and not hearing what they were saying as she went. Racked with guilt that maybe Challenger remembered her bad riding and hadn't forgiven her; fear that he might be ill. She hadn't wanted anything to do with the stupid animal in the first place; why did he have to come back? What had she done in this meeting Diane again? This was all so bloody stupid. She now had an overwhelming desire to burst into tears.

She slammed the front door and went up to her room. And to make it worse, no one followed her. Not that she wanted a deep heart to heart with anyone, but it would have been nice to tell them to disappear. No one came by that evening either. She was left to stew it all over. Getting nowhere. And this wasn't her fault; she had done nothing wrong. She hadn't even thought the flipping horse was alive, let alone want it back. Why did Dad think it such a good idea?

For once in so many years, she wished for her Mum. There would have been none of this if she hadn't been driven off the road by a drunken driver. No, her life would have been so different. Mum might have been horse obsessed and autocratic, but she could deal out a swift hug and unquestioning sympathy when needed; especially when you screwed up. Even if later, she would point out the truth of a matter. From nowhere, came the grief from the funeral, as fresh and painful as on the day. Joanna wept and felt so alone.

Later that evening, as if to add insult to injury, she looked out her window to find that they'd parked Challenger in the paddock right next to her end of the house. What was this, some sort of conspiracy to make her review her past and do something? But her life was OK; things were running smoothly and successfully; she was content.

Well, blast them all. Picking up her laptop, she looked for a last-minute deal for an all-in holiday somewhere hot and no horses. She booked a fortnight in Tunisia. The flight was the following day. Then she wrote an email to Ray and Diane.

'I've decided to take a break, there's not a lot to do for the next couple of weeks. I'm going to Tunisia for a bit of sun and R&R. I never wanted that horse back, and I think it must have something wrong with it. It's all yours Diane. Thank you all for your lack of support yesterday. You threw me into a situation that I had no way of dealing with. I thought the past was dealt with. I was happy until you raked it all up by doing this.'

Early next morning, Joanna packed and found her passport. She then deliberately left her laptop on full view in the kitchen - as if they would bother to look to see where she had gone anyway. Striding out of the house she shouted, 'stupid horse.' He rewarded her with another ears back grimace.

# FIVE

Well, girl, I think you done yourself proud, mused Joanna as she sat on the lounger, drink at one side, book in hand; hardly anyone on the beach and complete rest. Temperature pleasant and not scorching. Good!

For the first few days she had slept silly hours; maybe she had been more tired after the show than she had thought. Then she had surfaced and found the hotel child-free, just a little entertainment in the evenings, nothing organised. She could be as antisocial as she wanted. It was eating, drinking just a little, reading, swimming at least a kilometre in the pool to make up for the pigging out, and just avoiding reflecting on what had brought her here. Even better.

Now she had only three days left. A sense of impending doom filled her as she knew that she had to go home and face the music. Not so good. From nowhere, all of the repressed thoughts and emotions began to break over her. And being Joanna, for just a few minutes she let the negativity sweep, then she tried to make some order of things.

It was fine that Diane was there, it had to be. The decision had been made; there was no going back. She had to live with it all and that wretched horse. It was possible she had overreacted to the situation, but it had been thrust upon her. She would have to go back, apologise; get back to normal and keep on going on. There wasn't much choice, anyway. She would buy some apology pressies, and all would be fine. There was no need to keep on thinking about Mum; the look on Dad's face when she had stormed off. No more wondering why no one visited her. No. All best not thought about. She would be calm. Now she was rested, it would all appear quite different when she returned. She picked up her book. Those green eyes…

But it wasn't so easy a few days later on a drizzly, gloomy morning when she put her keys in the back door. The flat was dark and cold. She went around flipping switches, checking post, anything rather than go next door. Best to face things. She took a grip of herself and went through to the study, swinging hard on the Baize door, rubbing her hand on the mouldings as she did as a kid. Ray was bent over the accounts book and jumped when she spoke. For a second, he looked a bit nonplussed, then smiled,

'Glad to see you got back okay. Was the weather nice?'

'Wonderful, I just lounged and slept and ate and relaxed.'

'Good, good.'

'Look, I'm sorry about bolting. I was just overtired from the show and all the extra things happening…'

'No problem, one of those things.'

'Weren't you even worried about me?' She asked in a small voice.

'Not at all, you never have a password on your laptop, so I just looked up your booking!' So that had worked.

'Oh, right…so how've things been while I was away?' Even though Ray had done as Joanna had expected, she still wasn't happy.

'Pretty quiet, but we now must think about the Christmas do. The invites must go out soon. I've already had several invites for us to mince pies, and I accepted for you too. It seems to get earlier and earlier each year, just like the shops!'

'Right,' Joanna was perplexed; no recriminations, no telling off. Then she realised, maybe he didn't want a confrontation either. He wanted what she wanted; a quiet peaceful life, no complications. Relief swept over her.

'That guy from the archive office rang. He wants to bring someone over to look at our set-up and root around in the documents. His number's on the desk.'

'That sounds interesting, did he say who?'

'No, you'll just have to ring him.'

'How's Diane?'

'She's good. Had a few new clients, but with winter coming she says it'll close down gradually until spring. She's started talking about using the barn as an indoor school.'

Joanna rolled her eyes. 'I don't remember her being such a bulldozer when we were kids.'

'Probably because you were both flattening each other in your enthusiasm,' he grinned.

'Umm, could be,' Joanna forced a laugh, time to leave before this conversation developed any more.

'I'll see you in the office then unless we have anything planned today?'

'Not until later, then we're off to the Johnson's for drinks,' Ray peered at her again over his glasses.

'Right, so we'll go about 7?'

Shivering in the cold air, Joanna made her way to the stables, even calling, 'hello, you miserable old git,' to Challenger who just turned his quarters to her. He hadn't forgotten. Diane was cleaning tack.

'Hey, it's great you're back, did you have a good time? You look brown!' she said, smiling.

'It was just what I needed, a real rest. I'm back on track now, ready to get back to work.'

'Cool! I'm just starting to wind down for the season. The kids are back at school and sometimes it's too cold to stand around and do therapy unless we get a mild winter like last year.'

'What about all the Penelopes? Don't they still want to come?' asked Joanna remembering the Thelwell cartoon girls.

'Oh, they'll still come even if there's six foot of snow. But with only four horses I'm limited. There's not enough stables. If they're working they need to be in during the day. I've been talking to your dad about using the barn as well. It's so large I could put three boxes in and still have enough room for a therapy ring'

'Do you ever stop?'

'No, can't help it,' Diane laughed.

'Well, I don't see why you shouldn't use it, but it's not my area. You'll have to go on nagging Dad on that one.' No, she wouldn't get drawn in, even though she was grateful that Diane was letting things go.

'Are you going hunting this season?' Joanna asked trying to find something to talk about. 'The Boxing day meet still takes place at the pub even though it's trail hunting. I have heard that it's much faster and more dangerous as you're guaranteed a run and they pick the jumps.'

'I know, Ray told me. I did a bit in Wales, but these cobs aren't up to it.' There was a small silence. Joanna still feeling she needed to talk, and Diane wasn't giving any help.

'So, will you go back to Wales for Christmas?'

'No, Ray has invited us to the party, and for Christmas day so we'll be around.'

Joanna was staggered. What else had been going on while she was away?

'Um, we don't do much on Christmas day, we go to church and have a sing and feel happy, then eat leftovers from the party and open pressies that have come in from show customers. We don't bother otherwise.

Some years we have so much wine we don't have to buy any until next Christmas! Ever since Mum died, we haven't done Christmas day fully. It's been more nursing the party hangovers.' This didn't seem to put Diane off.

'Mum still does manic Christmas, so she'll be in your kitchen cooking turkey and all. You won't be able to stop her I'm afraid. When Dad was here, it used to be so over the top but wonderful. It's never been the same since then.' Diane looked weepy, so Joanna frantically searched again for another subject. She was saved as a car drew into the yard and a Penelope disgorged herself with a flurry of jodhpurs, hat and excitement.

As she walked back to the house Joanna realised she was relieved that it had all gone so well but also extremely puzzled that nothing had been mentioned about Challenger. It was if it had never happened. No comeback at all. It wasn't like her dad not to at least try to sort things or moan at her. But what the heck; why not brush it under the carpet? She had overreacted, and they in turn had realised she needed a break. Anyway, she wasn't going to try to bring it up if they weren't. Now there was Christmas and the mince pie month of drinks parties and socialising to look forward to.

Harry, the archive man arrived the next afternoon in response to Joanna's call. He brought with him a tall thin, middle-aged man who introduced himself as Tony the London manager. Joanna noticed that Harry was looking ill at ease. Quite unlike the cheerful guy who had so painstakingly guided her through the process of cataloguing and storing the documents. Joanna shook hands with Tony and led the way down the stairs through the repaired door. He stood and looked around.

'This looks well set up for a small collection. It was nice that for once that we didn't have to seek extra funding.'

Joanna's hackles went up. Was this an indirect jibe at her? We? She'd never met him before!

'Well it's quite unique as I said, Tony, to find documents that have been untouched for over a century and complete too. The diary entries about what Nelson got up to on his visits will cause a furore with the historians,' said Harry, wringing his hands. Tony grunted and began looking through the filing cases and boxes, at the computer; scrutinising everything closely. Somehow neither felt like adding to the comment. They watched. After a while, he shut a drawer and at last, smiled.

'My reason for wanting to visit, and I'm sorry Harry I couldn't say more until I'd checked. The reason is that some prat saw we had catalogued this with no one asking for funding of any sort. They thought there was some sort of dodgy dealing going on here. It's a control thing I suppose. They don't like private enterprise at HQ…'

'You mean like a bribe? For helping us with our collection? I only asked Harry in because I was worried that if we just put them in boxes, they might fall to bits!' interjected Joanna.

'And I'm glad you did. This is a fantastic job and a credit to you both.' Both Harry and Joanna began to plump up with a bit of pride.

'Now, Joanna you must come and work as a volunteer in the County Record Office. There is an opening in the New Year and I think you would gain a lot of ideas in how to use all this. We can teach you how to reply to enquiries because believe me they will begin in once Harry has put everything online.'

'I thought that was the end of it! I didn't realise I had more work to do, I thought he dealt with it all now. I was relieved everything was safe. Wow, that sounds interesting.' Joanna found she was saying the truth, not just placating. Both men were beaming now.

'When can I start?'

'I'll get an appointment for you to have an induction, and we'll go from there.'

There was a real feeling of bonhomie as Joanna led the men out, now making general small talk. Harry was back to his usual self and as he opened the door for his boss. Behind his back he gave her a double thumbs up signal and grinned. As soon as they had driven away, Joanna rushed to tell Ray. She found him yet again leaning over the fence watching Diane teach.

'You won't believe what they wanted! The main office is so delighted with our work they want me to go and do voluntary work! Then I can run our collection. I'll also find out more about looking after documents. Isn't that great! They came over because someone didn't like it all being done without funding.' Joanna was aware she was rattling on, and then she astonished as Ray turned and gave her a hug for the first time in years.

'That is amazing! I'm so glad, you put so much work into it last year!' he stepped back and smiled. 'Best news for ages.' They both stood and watched a Penelope getting her rising trot and the world was good.

The day continued with its surprises. That evening Joanna was beginning to collate all the information about last year's Christmas party when there was a knock at the door. Chloe was there with a tentative smile on her face.

'Hi Joanna. I was just, well wondering if you needed a hand with organising the party. Diane said you find it a huge last-minute rush and I'm a bit at a loose end with her out the house and there aren't the church groups here we had in Wales…' she paused for breath.

'Chloe come in and have a coffee. We can talk about it!'

She came in with a relieved smile and sat at the table while Joanna bustled about. Chloe started looking through the paperwork. Something was bothering Joanna. That was it. How did Diane know so much about their Christmas? Then before the kettle boiled came the first question.

'Why do you use these caterers from Southampton and that rubbish band from the University?'

Joanna handed over the cups. 'Well, I guess we must have put out for tenders or I looked around the internet for a good deal. Sometimes it works, sometimes it doesn't.'

'But why don't you get the pub to do the catering and bar any more?'

'I don't know,' Joanna thought for a moment. 'I guess it might have been the last tenant, he didn't do food and was a miserable git.'

'Have you met the new one?'

'You know we haven't! And he's been here over a year. We seem to be so busy with the show all year that we just don't get out and about much,' excused Joanna.

'Well, Diane and I have been down there several times. Did you know his wife does the catering? Their Sunday roast is to die for, and the place is so clean but homey. Why don't you get them to do it?'

'Maybe it's too near the time. People book Christmas parties in the summer now?'

'Rubbish. I know, we'll look through all this stuff and then we'll have supper there.'

Chloe then proceeded to argue the guest list, the waiting staff and the menu. By eight Joanna was aware that she was in the middle of a tornado, but she didn't mind. It was nice to have a woman to talk to. Diane was a friend but there was the blockage of the horses which always seemed to hold her back. Even when they were kids, Chloe had always been there with the horses. Although she had refused to ride, she was adept at holding reins and closing trailer ramps; more a friend than a mum.

Chloe was right about the pub. The new owner, Terry and his wife, Julie were pleasant and interested in doing the party. They had worked wonders on what had been a bit of a dump. Chloe and Joanna sat by a roaring fire; the bar and tables were now clean. There was no longer any smoking except outside and that made all the difference.

Chloe was right about the food too. The curry Joanna had was perfect; she would have signed them up then and there, but Chloe said just wait till they put it all in writing. Terry and Julie also knew of a good local band who was just starting out, i.e. their son and his mates. Joanna now found herself booked to hear them play on the following weekend.

The band passed the test, with Joanna, Chloe, Diane and Ray coming home that Friday night definitely worse for wear and a little deaf. The band could do all the standards for a party and some new stuff; if a little wobbly. But most people by the middle of the evening wouldn't notice, anyway.

Time slipped away in the usual routines of putting the old show to bed and beginning the new. Joanna and Diane kept a friendly, busy sort of distance between them, and suddenly the Christmas onslaught began. Yet Joanna found she enjoyed it more than ever before. Working with someone with new ideas, which were maybe sometimes wacky was fun. The most visible being the front of the house covered in fairy lights, but it looked amazing. Ray had never been much help; not into things like what colours shall we theme the decorations bit.

The two women cleaned, shoved furniture and argued over where the tree should be. Joanna had lost that one too. It was now in the hall decorated in the green and red theme. The buffet was now in the dining room; leaving the biggest room at the back of the house for dancing. The sitting room had the bar. It all made sense; why hadn't Joanna thought of this before? Keeping to tradition, being in a rut she surmised. Joanna felt a sense that it was as if the work with the show had cut them off a little from the local community, as Chloe insisted they got as much as possible nearby. It surprised Joanna just how much was on her doorstep.

It had been so nice just to chat about nothing in particular, drink a coffee and talk about the TV. Joanna realised that maybe her life was somewhat isolated and lacking in contact. Because of the drive to find a new sponsor for the cup, she and Ray ate more Mince pies than they had for a long time. They even made a scoring system for each do based on pies and booze. They saw little of Diane who seemed to have more and more clients with the horses despite her forebodings about the weather. She made it clear she couldn't be doing with organising parties. Joanna was relieved, one bulldozer was enough. There didn't seem to be a starting point for them to be the best friends they were. Maybe they wouldn't, but she was too busy to examine it closely.

# SIX

'Aren't we just the best?'

Diane and Joanna were dressed in new frocks ready for the Christmas party. Joanna had chosen a fifties style with a tightly waisted dress in light blue with matching high heels which set off her cascading blonde hair. Diane a slimline light brown with a flowing hemline.

'I think I can top that!' Chloe waltzed in, bursting out of a bright green, silk ball gown for once, not in cheesecloth. 'We're a flock of Peacocks!'

'Are we ready for the onslaught?'

'We are!'

All three linked arms and marched to the top of the stairs and were rewarded with a flash of light as Ray took their photo. Unfortunately, the staircase wasn't wide enough for all three. They giggled and took turns down. Chloe was first and found herself swept off her feet by Ray and given a twirl. Giddily she laughed. 'That was unexpected!' At which Ray presented her with a Christmas corsage to pin to her dress.

'That's just a small thank you for all your help with the organising. It's made such a difference to us all!'

Then it was Joanna's turn to be swung and pinned. She felt so happy that she could have yelled it out. Diane to her surprise got a kiss on the cheek from her dad.

'You wash up well too Ray!' said Chloe and pushed her arm through his. 'Let's hit the booze!' A glass of champagne had Joanna feeling even more in the party mood. The guests began to arrive. There were all the familiar faces from around the village and the farms, along with folks from further away who were involved in the show. It also seemed that there were more of the local people than in previous years. Had her feelings been right about the turn their lives had taken?

Harry from the archives turned up in a suit instead of the old jeans and jacket he wore for work. He washed up well too she thought. He couldn't be much older than her she realised. Oh, was there something in the air? She took in his brown eyes and curly hair and thought, yeah, you're actually OK. And you're stuck with me tonight as you don't know anyone!! Following Chloe's lead, she pushed her arm through his and gave him a big grin.

'The bar first?'

'Naturally!'

They met Diane looking lonely in the sitting room, so introductions were made, and the evening began its alcoholic spin. When the band started up, Joanna found Harry was a demon dancer. They spun and jigged and pogoed between nipping to the bar and padding the alcohol out with snacks from the buffet. She didn't keep Harry to herself either. He kept on being taken away by her school friends, the worst being Gloria. They did the old school dance to Mud's Tiger feet with a completely new swing.

As Gloria curtsied and handed him back to Joanna, she gasped for breath. 'I'm getting too old for all this, but that was magic. You better bring him to our New Year's party or I'll never speak to you again!'

Joanna was lambasted with invitations to parties after Christmas, and she accepted all; not so certain she would remember, but there was always WhatsApp. She had never realised there was such a social network in the area. What had she been doing the past few years? Diane was popular too, she even danced with Ray a couple of times. And Chloe? Boy, could she dance! She nearly had Ray off his feet in a jive as Joanna watched with great amusement. She then clocked someone making his way to her. It was Security man! There obviously was a case for having more parties as in shirt and tie even he looked good too. His manky hair had been cut back, and he looked thinner.

'May I have the pleasure?' His eyes transfixed her.

Joanna smiled. 'Of course! We may have met at embarrassing times of my life, but I don't know your name.' He formally gave his hand,

'Guy Brown at your service. No longer part of any security team!'

They laughed, and he spun her onto the floor. Joanna felt like a whirlwind had swung her away. He wasn't much of a dancer but had rhythm. The trouble was the music was at the shouting in each other's ear volume, so they didn't get much beyond the weather and what are you doing for Christmas. He was visiting friends in Southampton.

Then he disappeared as Harry came bounding up and swung her away. She now found his eagerness irksome. That was the thing with Harry she realised. He was shorter than her and that was an off-put, but maybe she could change her mind. Then the music slowed to a smooch, and it was difficult with her shoulders above his; he made up for it in drunken banter which had her giggling. It just felt, well, almost odd after Guy.

Out of the corner of her eye, Joanna saw Ray making the slow moves with Chloe. It looked so right that the idea crept into her head that maybe Chloe would be a great stepmother. Diane was being engulfed by one of the farm workers and grimaced as she went past.

It was the most wonderful evening thought Joanna as the last guest was taxied away at 3 am. Ray locked the front door and swayed a little.' I think that was the best party we've had for years, maybe we should employ Chloe to do it all for us. Happy Christmas!' He hugged her and they went their wobbly way to their beds.

Joanna awoke to the sound of the church bells coming from the village. For a moment she thought they'd slept in, but no, it was the early service. It was like something from a 1950s black and white film. Her nose picked up something. It was the smell of turkey, bacon and other festive goodies cooking. Chloe must be living up to her word of loving everything for Christmas. Great. That meant at least another hour in bed. She rolled over under the duvet.

'Wakey wakey!' In came a beaming Chloe with a mug of her ever-present coffee. 'Rise and shine, Christ is born, Peace to all men. It's Christmas and breakfast is ready.' Definitely a tornado. Joanna made her way to the shower with the coffee which was mind-blowing, full of chicory, caffeine and sugar. Within a few minutes, she was through the baize door to the main kitchen, wearing her favourite Christmas jumper. There was chaos everywhere apart from the red themed table where a repast needed eating. Joanna found that her hangover had gone, and she was hungry. Bacon and eggs from heaven! Ray and Diane came in and finally, Chloe came and sat down too. Christmas carols in the background; it could have been completely kitsch, but Joanna felt overwhelmed with the love and happiness that Chloe made with every gesture.

'Now, I've got everything prepared, it'll all go like clockwork, so we've plenty of time before church. We'll eat about about one o'clock. But I must announce this,' she cleared her throat dramatically. 'Today I don't wash up!'

'Darn,' said Ray. 'But I'm sure the girls will enjoy it. As lord of the manor, I will clear the table and serve and top up the drinks. That's my part.' There was a twinkle in his eye that Joanna hadn't seen for a long time. Comfortable laughter filled the kitchen, and the morning proceeded as Christmas dictates. They sent Chloe to watch the TV and cleared the kitchen together, then they all piled in the landrover for church. They all had on bad Christmas jumpers and found the Vicar was sporting one too. He made this the theme for his service, talking about Christmas traditions old and new; but that it didn't matter if love was entwined within it all. As they sang old songs and new, Joanna for once didn't shuffle her way sleepily through, but sang heartily. On the way out she was surprised that, so many people greeted her; many looking a little jaded still from the previous night. This hadn't happened for years and consolidated Joanna's growing worry that she and Ray had somewhere taken a wrong turn in this community. They weren't the lords of the manor but the biggest landowner and employer in the area. She must talk to him about this all later.

Back home, they had to pull Chloe away from basting to the presents. There were a lot from show people as usual, so they opened these first. Looking at the heap of chocolates and booze Chloe looked up.

'You know, this is all a bit OTT. What do you do with all this stuff?'

'Well Joanna eats most of it!' laughed Ray. 'Seriously, the wine goes in the cellar and we use the chocs and the other bits and pieces as pressies. If the dates are okay, they go for raffles and prizes.'

'Don't you think we could donate some of this to the homeless place I took all the leftovers to?'

'You did what?' exclaimed Ray. They all looked at him apprehensively. 'What a flaming good idea. When did you find the time, did you sleep at all last night?'

'It wasn't too difficult, I packed it up and Jenny dropped it off just after two!'

'Chloe, you're amazing! But the booze, is that a good idea?'

'They're not all alcoholics, and maybe the volunteers would like a thank you.'

'Chloe, I bow down to you!' And Ray did to more laughter.

'Now in our tradition, one pressie each at a time.' That didn't work as they all now scrambled under the tree for the personal ones. Joanna found herself with the usual bath stuff from Ray; he had the usual aftershave. When she opened hers from Diane, she found a pair of brightly coloured leggings, but when she looked closer, she found they were jodhpurs. For a split second, she knew she had a choice. Another hissy fit or laughter? Laughter won.

'You just don't give up do you?' She said for the umpteenth time.

'I was always a trier!' Joanna had given Diane some smart Ikea cushion covers to match the flat. Chloe gave Joanna some books, and again there was another split second. Did she chuck the Bible and the self-help books? No, again, she managed to laugh, 'Like mother like daughter!' She had given Chloe some enormous, colourful earrings that she knew Chloe would love. She did, and put them straight in and swung her head. Joanna didn't clock what the others gave each other in the scrimmage as she concentrated on her booty. Then, as usual, there was the sense of disappointment when the last was opened and so much glamour was just a heap of scrambled paper.

Chloe appeared with eggnogs, which Joanna had never tried and found hers far nicer than expected. Chloe banned everyone from the kitchen and sent them to lay the table. There was still some mess from the previous night, but they used leftover napkins, bits of tinsel and the little Christmassy decorations that had furnished the plates. They stood back to admire,

'It's totally naff but I love it,' said Joanna as she took a photo. 'It all seems to go so well with the family china!'

Then as in so many houses at that time of the day, roast turkey and all the trimmings, followed by an enormous pudding were eaten and enjoyed along with several bottles of the better wine. What was merry became merrier still.

Ray pushed his chair back and eased his belt buckle. 'Chloe, I don't know how to thank you. That was the best Christmas meal I've eaten in my life. I now propose a toast. To the Queen of Christmas at Hazeley manor, Chloe!'

They raised glasses to a blushing Chloe.

'Your turn now!' Chloe took her glass and raised it.

'To old friends becoming new. Fresh starts and new horizons. The Blessings of Christ who is born to bring peace to us all!'

Glasses were filled and again Ray waved to get their attention.

'Now, I think that was the most wonderful and appropriate toast. And now I have an announcement to make. Danny come over here.'

Danny, Danny? thought Joanna. I've never heard her called that before and she felt a sudden premonition of something odd; but before she could process the thought, Ray was off.

'Not so many years ago, all of our lives were changed through different tragedies. We lost Mia, and you lost Duncan. It led to great changes in our loves and ways, but we're all together again.'

Joanna now wondered if he would propose to Chloe; neat.

'We've changed and grown older, if not wiser,' he smiled placatingly thought Joanna. 'Our lives are made complete through our relationships with loved ones. When we lose someone, we may think that it is the end of it all. But this year's events have brought a new love into my life, in a way I've never thought possible. You may see hurdles in the way of this, but I'm sure you'll see they aren't big jump off jumps. Yes, this autumn I fell in love again like I was twenty all over again. And this love is returned!'

Joanna saw Chloe's face was a shade of green; she looked like something from a horror film.

'And now it's time to tell you all so you can share our joy. Not long ago, I asked Danny to become my wife, and she agreed. Please share in our new joy and the excitement that we've found together!' He raised his glass. Joanna and Chloe looked at each other, beyond the power of speech, and dutifully lifted their glasses. Unwittingly giving over that they were condoning the whole thing.

'Now Danny here is the ring to cement our engagement.' Ray took a box out of his pocket and slipped the ring onto Diane's finger. She was beaming from ear to ear; neither of the lovers paid any attention to their audience. They didn't pick up straight away on the strained air.

'Mum aren't you happy for me?' Diane asked. Chloe appeared to pull herself physically together.

'It's a bit of a shock, I had no idea. Congratulations.'

The ring was waved in front of her. And then at Joanna, who was so numb that she felt like a puppet going through the actions. 'It's lovely!' was the best she could mutter. The lovebirds had only eyes for each other as they admired the ring. Chloe caught Joanna's eye and beckoned with her head towards the kitchen.

'Right, let's get some of this cleared up.' She said loudly and grabbed some plates, exiting as quickly as possible with Joanna on her tail. She dropped the plates noisily on the counter. 'Come on, we're out of here, let them clear the mess up.'

# SEVEN

The two put on wellies and coats and bolted out the back door. They took the path up through the oak wood without a word and strode up the hill to the viewpoint. Both were panting when they reached there, the heavy meal not helping. It wasn't too cold for a December day, so they sat cooling on the bench for a few minutes in bewildered silence.

'I never saw that one coming,' said Chloe. 'And, I've got no grounds to complain. The age difference is not that bad, Ray was younger than Mia, and Diane is older than you if you see what I mean. There are only about ten years between them; it's nothing these days. But you don't know all of what we went through after Duncan's death. I'm sure she didn't give you the X rated version.' Joanna was content to listen; it stopped her thinking.

'When we were taken away, we knew he had gone. But with the not knowing when or where in some ways it made our grief worse-the very thing he was trying to avoid. We had to fight to have a private service for ourselves, and that helped me.

Diane held it all in. As many teenagers do, she tried to find a father substitute in any man that came by. When she got into the show jumping, I thought she had found a direction for her energy and pain, but no, she slept her way around some of the biggest names in the business. I tried never to criticise her; held her when it all went wrong, but there's a limit to how much a daughter will stand from a mother.

Then by chance, she went off to do some of this equine therapy or whatever current name it has. I went with her and watched; it was amazing. They put her in a pen with all these horses and told her to pick the one which she thought was the best and bring it back.

They did warn us that horsey people often aren't so good with it as the horse stuff is easy. However, at first, she couldn't pick, then she went around them one by one, talking to them and trying to make a decision – there were a lot of horses about twenty I think. After about fifteen minutes they called her over and asked her what was going on, could she relate it to her life, as she hadn't picked one in the time.

She broke down. I couldn't believe how walking around with a few horses got through to her where I couldn't. She saw straight away how it paralleled her sleeping around; looking for some quality that wasn't there. It opened the whole can of worms, and she, at last, agreed to have grief counselling as well as more of this therapy.

Then she trained to do it as you know. There may have been more men, she won't tell me things any more. I should trust her. Do you think Ray knows what he's let himself in for? I'm scared she'll be all loving, and then when she finds he's a man, not her father she'll bolt again. It was such a shock. I was so rude, we shouldn't have walked out. What have I done? I must go back. Maybe, at last, he is the one for her. Can you handle this? Are you coming back with me?'

'No, I guess I need a little time to think. I won't be long, you go.'

Chloe was gone in an instant, leaving Joanna staring into the biggest, blackest hole. She had never felt so alone in her life. It had been grim when Mia died, but she and Dad had sort of knocked a life out as she grew up. She had made her career with the show and all it entailed. But now the mat was truly pulled from under her feet. He hadn't said a word to her about it, not a hint, nor a change, nothing.

Or had there? When he hadn't taken off after her about the horse? As a child he had always been there for her, the first boyfriend break up, girly class problems, exams, they had always chatted things through. It had been a companionable, happy childhood and teenage for her, despite the lack of her mother. Together, they had worked together building the show up to the national event it now was.

This was the ultimate betrayal from someone who she had been trying to see as her new best old friend and buddy despite their differences. If Dad had asked Chloe she would have been overjoyed. The bitch. Had she come here to take Dad from her? Had this been the plan all along? Was she behind Joanna being left alone after the horse thing? Had Dad been so besotted that he couldn't even tell her himself? What had she done wrong that she had to be treated like this? Why did it have to be so secret and so quick? There must be something wrong. This was not of her doing, and now he would be so besotted. She would have no one. Huh, the cow would be her stepmother.

That finished Joanna, and she howled out her pain. Some bloody Christmas this was, and it had all seemed so perfect. She would now be the outsider as no doubt Chloe would organise the wedding. She felt her aloneness acutely; there was no comfort in any corner. Diane would be his partner in running the show.

Bridesmaid? That made her burst into tears again. How could she even walk into the house? Then she realised that she didn't have to. She could go into her flat through the field and her back door. They would never know she was home. If things were as she suspected, they wouldn't even miss her.

In the growing darkness, Joanna walked down the hill and like a criminal she checked out that there was no one in the yard and made her secret entrance. She crept through and shoved an armchair in front of the baize door. This was more for her own benefit but it helped.

In the sitting room, she drew the curtains, lit the fire and found some of her share of the wine and chocolates. Then it was a trashy film until the wine knocked her out and she slept. In what seemed like the middle of the night she was woken by someone tapping on the window. Blearily, she got up from the sofa before her thoughts kicked in and went to see who it was. Chloe was beckoning, so she went around to let her in. It was all flooding back along with a headache; but it was too late.

'Morning Joanna! We missed you last night, did you go out? We thought you had gone out when you didn't come in. I had imagined you might join us after your time out. I think it will be fine! We had quite a little party in the end,' she beamed at her. 'It was a huge shock but isn't it wonderful! Do let's be happy for them. I can't still quite believe it myself.'

She had bulldozed in and was putting the kettle on. 'And you know her so well. You'll be like real sisters rather than in-laws!' She rattled on without pausing for breath, and Joanna began to get caught up in the enthusiasm. Could it be she was overreacting? Maybe it would be a good thin; , perhaps she had jumped to conclusions, it might be OK.

'Its fine Chloe, I'm glad for them.' At that moment she felt it. Quickly sweeping all her misgivings and hurt under the rug and standing firmly on it. She would stick with this, it seemed the only sane way. There was no chance for a real discussion though.

'Fantastic! Right here's your coffee. Be sharp, we haven't much time.'

'For what?' Was the wedding this morning?

'It's the Boxing day meet in the village and we're all going down, come on.'

Joanna found herself rushing about getting dressed and within minutes piling in the landrover. She ended up in the back with Chloe as Diane was firmly in the front. Ray leaned back and grinned.

'Morning dear, everything in order? Did you have a nice chat with Chloe?' he smiled. 'I'm on top of the world this morning!'

'Oh, that's, um, great.' The sinking feeling was back again. Would she always be on the back seat from now on?

At the meet, Ray and Diane started telling people, and Joanna watched the differing reactions. Some seemed genuinely pleased, some taken aback, others just polite. Getting bored with the theme and sipping her drink she looked around at the field. She had hunted herself long before it had changed to trail hunting, so she was mildly interested.

There were certainly more people about. The horses looked far more athletic than the cobs and heavy hunters she remembered. Kids were now toting body protectors under their jackets, as were a lot of the adults. In my day she thought sagely, you fell off and broke your neck and got on with life!

Her glance caught a striking palomino stallion who was obviously bottled up. He skittered about at the back of the green. He was held down with martingale and a nasty looking bit that Joanna had never seen the like of. But his rider looked complacent, even grinning as the horse pretended to be scared of a blowing crisp packet. For a split second, she wanted to be there on that horse. Then remembered times when sitting on Challenger before an event was like sitting on a time bomb.

Adrenalin or not, she was glad she wasn't riding today. In fact, she no longer had any desire to belt about the place, eyes streaming in the cold! She shivered and was glad to see the Hunt moving off. Now they all decamped into the Pub. This was a token following, no driving around the countryside. After all, it was a trail and those in the know knew where the best places were; not like the past said an old boy as Ray bought him a drink. Joanna found herself sat next to Diane and unable to find a thing to say to her.

'Are you all right, Joanna, you seem a little aloof today? Is everything okay?' Diane was right in her face.

'Oh, I'm fine. It's just taking a while for everything to sink in.'

'Yes, I guess we'll have a lot of things to chat about in the next couple of months. After all, May isn't that far off,' she said excitedly. 'May! Yes, didn't Ray tell you? We set the date for the third Saturday. It won't be a big do; and we'll have time for our honeymoon before it all gets busy.'

Joanna didn't have the courage to ask whether Diane meant the show or the therapy work.

'I won't insult you with asking you to be a bridesmaid, and you're not married, but would you be my Maid of Honour? There's no other role I can think of!'

Joanna gulped. 'Um, well yes, I suppose so, providing I don't have to wear a blancmange!'

'No, no, we'll find something that you can wear again and that fits in with the colour scheme. Oh, it'll be such fun. Ray was worried about all this as a shock for you. But you had some time out last night and you're great now, aren't you? After all, we're old mates and it's just so perfect. I've never met a man like him!'

Joanna felt like she had been kicked in the chest by a large angry carthorse and for the moment couldn't speak. She managed a nod and was relieved that Diane took it all at face value and turned back to Ray. Steamrollered and kicked. This was so real.

After all Chloe had said about Diane's adventures, was this going to happen? Would it last? She'd never seen Diane like this. She had seemed a completely different person; bubbling and excited. That might be natural when you got engaged. Joanna remembered Gloria swinging her ring around and bursting into tears when she had told Joanna but mainly because she had thought Brian would never ask.

Joanna realised the worst thing was that she'd lost her dad forever. Nothing would be the same; he was in Diane's grip. She felt like she was dying inside, she'd lost him. There would be no more companionable evenings slobbing in front of the TV, no more cosy chats. No more working together on the show as no doubt, Diane would muscle in on that one too. A small ray of hope was that Chloe was right and Diane would lose interest before the wedding. But May was so soon. Then Dad would be hurt. What could she do? Nothing except grin and bear it and maybe one day, she might get a chance to tell Dad how she felt. Not that it would change much, would it? She was torn between trying to be happy for Dad, then worrying for the long term of it all and realising she didn't actually like the Diane of today. But she had to be pleased for them. She gulped her drink.

Chloe's phone rang with its loud ridiculous tone and she went out to answer. Before she reached the door, she turned around with a broad grin on her face. It seemed like all in the pub listened to her conversation.

'John, that's fantastic! When? Oh, for how long? That's a shame. Where? That's do-able. Can I call you back on this number? Which hotel did you say? Right got it. Speak soon.' Her face was aglow. 'John's flying from Europe to the States on the 29th, but he has a few days stopover in London. Not enough time to get down here, but we could all meet up at his hotel for a couple of nights. What do you think?'

'Really? Uncle John? When did we last see him, Mum?'

'Must be all of two years ago. You know what he's like, married to his work. But let's go, we could do a show as well and some shopping??' Chloe cocked a con-spiritual eyebrow at Diane. Joanna's spirits lifted. Thank you, God, that was a quickly answered prayer. Dad and I can have a chat and we can get things straight. I can sort all this out with him and we can move forward.

'And Ray, you'll just love him when you meet him. He more than likely won't make the wedding. You can never rely on him. He'll be so excited to hear all our news!'

Joanna was back in the pit again, and there was worse to come. Diane had a pensive look on her face.

'It's not that simple. There are the horses to consider. While they're all out and rugged, they need checking daily. Hay put out. If the weather takes a turn for the worse, then they must come in as they're clipped...'

'Couldn't one of the kids from the village do the job?'

'None of them are old enough.'

'Um, Joanna, I don't suppose you could help us out?' Diane turned spaniel eyes on Joanna.

'Me? You must be kidding!' She was aware of three sets of pleading eyes boring down on her. 'I haven't been near a horse in years. Why should I do this?'

'But it'll just mean a trip up the field once a day. If something goes wrong, we're only in London. Pleeeease Joanna. I haven't seen Uncle John in years,' Diane pleaded. 'It's not as if you need to meet him.'

Ouch! 'But I've got plans. I'm planning on staying with Gloria. She's having a party…'

'You could go to her any time, and there'll be other parties,' said Ray, doing the look over his glasses. Joanna felt five years old again, thwarted, given platitudes when really, she had no choice. She was firmly backed into a corner.

'Oh, I suppose so. But I want everything left ready for all possibilities, Vet numbers, feed, and I'm not poo picking.'

'No, we don't do that in the twenty acre. I'll show you everything in the morning. Thank you!' Joanna was engulfed in a stiff hug from Diane; the last thing she wanted in the world. When she looked over her shoulder her father looked as though he was consciously avoiding her gaze. Joanna felt worse, something wasn't right.

# EIGHT

Over lunch, the conversation went on and on about what they would do in London, with Joanna feeling steadily more and more alienated. When she tried to take part in the conversation, Diane would butt in; questioning her or dismissing what she said. It was a relief when they bundled back into the landrover and drove home. Joanna made her escape; she just wanted to nurse her grievances with more wine and chocolates. Brigit Jones, eat your heart out she thought angrily as she stoked up the fire and put on another DVD.

Yet it seemed that it would be straightforward with the horses when Diane showed her the bales of hay stacked behind the field shelter. Easy. Diane's gratefulness seemed genuine which tempered Joanna's anger. Even so, she was glad when they drove out of the yard with cheerful waves and see you soons.

Joanna found it a blissful relief to be free of them. Their constant presence and cheerfulness just ground against her turmoil. She stood in the yard and felt that the air was getting colder, maybe a frost was coming. There was an odd sort of metallic smell too. Best get more logs later she thought.

A sudden sense of wickedness filled her: with the house empty, she would have a snoop! The ground-floor rooms had no interest, they were still filled with the remnants of Christmas. The sitting room was altered by the bits and pieces left by Chloe and Diane. She noticed a laptop left running and lost against the temptation to look. It was obviously Diane's as the screensaver had a horse on it. She sort of accidentally touched the screen and found a weather forecast programme running. Did she have the courage to small it and look at emails and things? No, she didn't want to know Diane's little secrets. She had enough to deal with. She left it to sort itself out and the battery go flat. No one would suspect.

Upstairs was the thing. She hadn't been up here since she took on her own wing. The biggest surprise was to find that the room her parents had shared was being used by Chloe; the Bibles and her snazzy clothes a big give away. When had Dad moved out? The furniture was the same, with the big bed where the three of them had cuddled when she was little. That hurt, but maybe that was better than Diane occupying it. She went to the biggest room and found ample evidence that her dad and Diane weren't waiting for the ceremony. She seemed to have a lot of stuff in the room. Had she really needed so much just for over Christmas?

In disgust she slammed the door, it was sick; it was wrong. Why did she think this was such a good idea? What if they had forgotten something and came back? No, her main snoop was to see her old room and they couldn't moan at her for that. It felt like sort of touching something safe. Her bed was still covered with the Take That quilt and the walls with their posters. Her pony books were still on the shelf. It was like she'd just walked out. Well, I suppose I did she thought.

She found some surprises in the cupboard. Her big yard jacket, too large for her then, she now found a good fit. That would do for seeing to the nags. At the back of the cupboard was her treasure box of things she hadn't wanted then, but couldn't part with; photos, diaries, the inevitable rosettes, and more old pony books. When had she found time to read them? She picked it up for a look through later. As she went downstairs, she could hear wind beginning to whistle around the chimneys; time to get the wood in.

Outside the wind was now roaring in the beech trees at the top of the hill. Joanna shivered despite her jacket. It was colder, but the horses would be all right; they were grazing on the lower ground where the field was sheltered from the wind.

After hauling in lots of wood, Joanna feasted on leftovers in the main kitchen, then shut all the curtains and went into her own side. She passed a happy afternoon reading several of the pony books, which she found she remembered almost word for word. They made her feel happy and secure as she airbrushed out all her negativity of the moment and went into the past. One book had Diane's name scrawled inside. Funny, where things seemed so wrong now, it had seemed so right when they had shared these books. Maybe pony books are forever Joanna mused. She didn't feel ready for the treasure box yet. It was getting dark and as she went to find a bottle of wine, she glanced out of the window.

'OH NOOOOO!' Snowflakes were falling, and the ground already had a covering. Now she'd have to get the horses in. No way was she mucking out for Diane, but she had an idea. Nevertheless, lots of choice expletives came to mind as she trudged to the barn.

At least the electricity was on for the lights. There were bales of straw that could be spread and more hay that could go in the round feeder from when the young stock had been in there. The automatic drinker just needed turning on, so no need to use the loose boxes.

She went into the tack room but found no torch for her trip up to the field. There might be one upstairs. To her surprise, the flat was very, very moved out of. Just how long had Diane been living with Dad, why had it been so secret? What a waste of Ikea. No time for that now. There was a torch in the electrical cupboard, and in the dying light, she made her way up the field.

The snow bit into her face, so it was a to see that as Diane had promised, the ropes were tied to the fence.

No haltering up, just leading them in. Five ropes? Oh no, Diane had conveniently forgotten the main issue. How was she ever going to get near Challenger to bring him in? He'd kick her head in first. Well, he could just die of cold, the stupid animal. The ponies seemed to think they should be indoors and were standing by the gate, but there was no sign of Challenger.

She swiftly clipped the ropes on and let the gate swing open, maybe misery guts would follow. It wasn't so bad. She'd led loads of ponies before and in their eagerness to be in, the four marched towards the lights. In the barn, she let go and they took themselves in.

Their rugs were soaking from the earlier rain and now the snow, so they had to come off. Joanna remembered the smell of wet rugs and horse as if it was yesterday. She slung the rugs over the boarding at the back and slamming the door behind her and went to find the stable rugs. The four ponies were soon warmly rugged, but one large blue rug was unused. She knew she would now have to go back up the field.

The snow was heavier now and the torch less effective in the darkness but at least she had her warm jacket. Joanna couldn't pick Challenger out at all, even though she called and called. Then it struck her that he was in the field shelter, right at the top of the field. She trudged and slipped her way up. There he was in the dry, but the snow was starting to blow in. She called his name, and he looked at her; for a split second their eyes met, and his head snaked out to make a vicious bite. Joanna lost her temper.

'Just for once in your stupid life, you, stupid daft horse, let me help you. Otherwise, you just might freeze to death, you idiot!' She yelled, letting out all the emotion of the past few days and then added a few more swear words on top. To her surprise, he stopped his snaking and just stood there. Amazing. She clipped the rope on and tugged hard. The two of them slithered their way to the barn. He even stood to have his rug changed. But as she turned to leave, his head snaked again.

'Don't even think about it.'

He stopped, turned his quarters and mooched off to the hay. Heaving a sigh of relief, Joanna locked the barn and slipped her way home.

She thawed out in a deep, hot bath and began to think about whether she should call London and ruin their stay. Maybe she wasn't quite that mean, and she wouldn't give them the satisfaction of thinking she couldn't cope. No, she would play the saint when they came back and that would make them feel doubly guilty. Sorted. But was it? Something was worrying her at the back of her mind. Then it came. The laptop was on a weather programme. The bitch! She had known the snow was coming and had left anyway without a word. Was she hoping that Joanna would make a mess of it and make herself look a failure? Was she trying to make Joanna look useless? Come back and take it all over like some sort of wicked stepmother?

Was it sheer vindictiveness? Was that why no one had even rung Joanna to see how things were? Was Diane just so in love she wasn't thinking straight? Joanna snorted into her glass. One thing for certain, she was now going to have some sort of retribution. The worm was turning. She would be sly too, she'd hold her knowledge about Diane's duplicity back in case she needed some real ammunition.

In the next couple of days, Joanna and Challenger held an armed neutrality. She didn't go near him and he ignored her. The barn was nicely dirty too; served Diane right. Joanna fed the horses early in the morning on the day everyone was due back, and in her mood of revenge was glad to see some nice stable stains on the rugs.

The snow was still holding its own, having laid a couple of inches. She had half expected a phone call to say they would wait in London for the roads to be cleared. The news had been full of the traffic chaos.

Joanna was still a little on edge as she shut the door and slipped her way along the ice back indoors. She kept herself busy, doing some unheard of housework to stop herself from reflecting too much. Another note and bolting straight off to Gloria's this morning would be counterproductive. Gloria had agreed and clucked in the right way, egging her on to come and party. But Joanna had been ignored before, so they weren't going to get away with that again. She would keep to her convictions.

It was with relief that she heard the car pull up into the yard and the slamming of doors and clattering around next door. Five minutes passed, then half an hour, then three quarters. This was too much for her, they were being horrible. As she went into the hall, she saw a pile of colourful, luxurious plastic bags from big name stores and her heart lurched. How she would have loved some shopping. Excluded again. Gritting her teeth, she went into the kitchen and found Chloe creating something on the cooker.

'Hi, Joanna!' She was engulfed in a huge Chloe hug. 'We had such a wonderful time, London was amazing.' Joanna stiffened and pulled back, she didn't want yet another meaningless Chloe embrace.

'Mum,' came Diane's voice from upstairs.' I need your help with unpacking this.'

'Just a minute Joanna, don't go, I'll be back.'

Partially comforted, Joanna waited. Then all three came thundering downstairs. She was given the account of how great it was to see John, the shopping, the posh hotel and the show they took in. After a while, they ran out of juice and looked expectantly at Joanna. She looked back. Finally, Ray said, 'So how was it here, the snow looks fantastic. The roads were cleared quickly in London, which was a surprise.'

'Yes, it has snowed a bit,' said Joanna with her best sarcastic tone. 'I was left in a snowstorm to bring in all those flaming horses on my own. They're still in now, and

I'm not doing any more with them. Enjoy your mucking out.' Joanna now exploded. 'Did it not connect that if there was snow in London that it was here too, and I might need some help? Did any of you bother to ring me and see how I was getting on? '

Diane looked pale but said nothing.

'But you could have rung us, Diane said you were fine and not to worry,' said Ray in a placating voice.

'Why should I? You all took off without a second thought. You're all so self-centred and selfish. No one even thought to ask if I even wanted to come despite whether I could or not. Shouldn't you at least have checked up on your precious nags when the snow came? No. You come swanning back, not one of you even puts your head around the door to say Hi. I don't know what I've done to get all this dross from you, but I've had enough.'

'Come on Joanna be reasonable,' said Diane. Joanna gained some self-control.

'Oh, I can be reasonable. So reasonable that when I need time off from the office in the New Year to go and work in the Record office, Dad, you're not going to moan at me. So reasonable that you can find another mug to be your Maid of Honour, Diane. I'm now off to see some people who I can call friends. They bother about what I'm up to, how I'm feeling and even seem to like my company a bit. I'll see you all on January 2nd when I come back to work.'

Joanna flounced out of their astonished quiet and left through the baize door. No one came after her as she expected. Another exit and nothing resolved. But whatever, Joanna was off to party the New Year in and party she did. It was a round of friends' houses and their kids, catching up, dancing, drinking and just putting it all behind her. On her return late one night, she didn't even bother to go into the other side of the house. She fell into bed and into a party exhausted sleep. The fun had put all into perspective and she just wanted to get on with life.

# NINE

The office on the edge of the village was in the old blacksmith's forge. It had been altered and air-conditioned, but every time Joanna opened the door she was sure she could smell hot metal and hear the clink of iron on iron. She opened the windows and let a bit of fresh air in. Then she checked the coffee supplies and made a list for the village shop. It was good to be on track again. There was a pile of post to sort out, so she switched the computers on for everyone and started opening envelopes. The doorbell rang as Sheila, one of the two secretaries came in.

'Happy New Year,' Joanna beamed. 'Ready for the onslaught?'

'Just about! Still recovering from the party at the pub, it was a real humdinger. You should have seen your dad and Diane. Boy they can rock-and-roll!' Sheila smiled. 'We missed you. It didn't seem right without you.'

The stab of jealousy that Joanna felt was replaced with pleasure; someone had missed her,

'I had a long-standing invite at Gloria's, and when I finally got there, we did a bit of rock and rolling too,' she grinned. 'Right now, do you want to do emails or post while I get supplies?' The two got down to work and by coffee time began to make some sense of it all. The accounts for the previous year were nearly ready to be sent away, and the draft schedule too. All the work in the autumn had paid off. Jenny arrived bearing cakes to go with the coffee and the three sat down in comfortable familiarity in the back room.

'Your dad's late, he's usually breathing down our necks. I suppose it's being in love,' said Jenny. 'Are you excited about the wedding?'

'Well it was all sudden, but yes,' said Joanna trying to be tactful if only for herself. 'There's still a lot to sort out and do!'

At that moment Ray burst into the office. 'Morning everyone, sorry I'm late.' He was beaming.

'Joanna, I'm going to have to tear you away. I've just had confirmation that the farm shop wants to take over the sponsorship of the County cup. They've invited us to lunch. Grab your coat, ladies, is everything oaky?'

'Nothing we can't cope with!' they laughed, and Joanna followed Ray's wake out to the landrover.

'Shouldn't we have taken the Jag or I wear my heels and suit for this?'

'Have you been to their place? It's a farm in the back of beyond, down miles of mud. No, it'll be very informal. Did you have a good New Year?'

'Brilliant. I caught up with everyone and boogied the night away.'

'Great, we had fun too. We need to catch up properly. How about afterwards we go to the Church Arms?'

'That sounds great.'

Joanna felt like the past few months had never occurred. All was back to normal and while keeping off the subject of the wedding, they chatted about the plans for this year's show and it felt good. For the first time, she felt happy for Ray; that he was happy made her happy. That had to be enough. Diane was another thing, but that thought she shoved under the table.

The farm was indeed in the middle of nowhere but was a thriving business. They were shown around the greenhouses, fields and the animal units. All very impressive. Martin was telling them about their plans to expand when a large hairy black dog came bouncing in and greeted Joanna and Ray like long-lost friends.

'She's escaped her puppies again and although she's not feeding them, they all live in the barn at night, in a run during the day. The two that remain are a real pair of live wires. Into everything, can't wait to find them a home,' Martin grinned at them. 'Don't suppose you fancy one?'

'We don't have time with the wedding and everything,' Ray said firmly. At which point, as if rehearsed the two puppies, came bounding in looking for Mum. They were both also black, but short coated and slim like whippets.

'We suspect Dad was the dog from the pub, but he denies it!' Both puppies made a beeline for Joanna who crouched down to accept a barrage of licks, whimpers, nips and squeaks of excitement.

'How old are they?'

'Four months. The other two went to family and I've just been too busy to put an ad in the paper or anything.'

'They're so cute! Are they both girls?'

'No, one of each. If you look, the boy has a white chest, and she has white feet.' The puppy obligingly lay on her back and waved them in the air.

'So sweet!' said Joanna.

'Don't even think about it, Joanna!' laughed Ray, which was possibly the worst thing he could have said. She didn't reply, but in her subconscious she was buying dog baskets, feeding bowls, putting a fence on the garden. They were lying at her side in the office and she was taking long healthy walks. Who was Ray to say what she could and couldn't do any more? She had her own money and flat; she wasn't a kid anymore. She kept quiet as they finished the tour and went in for lunch.

They feasted royally  on products from the shop and feeling completely stuffed, took coffees into the office where the contract was signed. A long partnership was toasted, and it felt like something great was starting afresh for the show. In a pause, Joanna spoke up.

'Martin are you serious about the puppies?'

'Well we can't keep them forever, they need a home and training, why are you interested in one?'

'Yes, I am,' she said resolutely avoiding Ray's gaze.

'Well they should be in the garden run, they are supposed to be there in the day, let's go and see.'

Ray looked daggers at Joanna as they walked out.

'You're not serious, are you?'

'Why not? I have the place and time, and I can afford it. They can sleep under the desk in the office.'

'THEY?'

'Calm down Dad, they'll keep each other company.'

The two puppies began wriggling and barking as soon as they saw people. Joanna didn't care what Ray said, she was in love. Martin let them out of the run and they went immediately to Joanna.

'So, which one would you like?'

'Well, as I can't decide, and they're such a pair, could I have both?' Joanna heard Ray's under breath moan.

'Wow, are you sure? Have you had dogs before, I must do the responsible owner bit!?'

'We had a labrador until about five years ago.'

'Well, but puppies? They can be very destructive.'

'I remember Max when he was little. I'm sure I can cope. Have they been vaccinated?' she asked in a way to prove she knew what she was doing.

'Wormed, but vaccinated not, you must take them to the vets as soon as possible once they're off the farm.'

'And here's the crunch, how much do they cost? Joanna was reckoning how much cash was in her purse.

'Oh, right, nothing! They're giveaways at this age. They aren't cuddly and cute so much and have already begun to grow. As I said, I am having trouble finding a home for them.'

'Wow, that's fantastic, thank you… Oh, do you have an old blanket or rug that smells of home for their first night?'

'I expect there's something stinky in the barn, let's look.'

They followed Martin back to the barn with the two pups bounding and leaping around them. Ray held Joanna a little back,

'You do realise I'm getting married in a few months,' he hissed.

'And I'm not. Back. Off.'

And he did as Joanna was handed a very smelly rug and they went to put it in the landrover. There were more thank yous; Joanna promising that they would meet again at the show and she'd let Martin know how they got on. She climbed into the back, and Martin passed one wriggler up so that the other wanted immediately to follow.

'Hang on a minute, I'll get you a bag of their food, so their tums don't get upset,' and he disappeared.

'I think you'll find that all the old dog stuff is in the storeroom on your side. That'll tide you over until you can shop,' came a placating offer from Ray.

'Thanks Dad,' Joanna placated back. 'They'll be fine.'

'Hmmph, we'll see.'

Martin handed a bag through the window and they waved again as they drove off. It was soon very clear that the pups had never been in a vehicle before and they proceeded to be sick both ends all the way home. Even with all the windows open, the air was thick. Joanna realised her catch up with Ray was out the window, but she didn't care. There was so much to think about, yes, maybe it was a rush decision and she should have sorted things out and gone back in another couple of days; she wasn't going to admit that! The air was also thick with

Ray's silent disapproval. Back home, he parked close to the back door and handed Joanna the keys.

'You can bring it back around the front when you have cleaned, disinfected and de-smelled it,' and he stomped off.

Joanna lurched out of the back and began to realise her problems might just be beginning. How could she get both indoors without one escaping? She shut them in behind her, which left two puzzled faces looking out the landrover window. She ran in, opened the door to the kitchen and ran back. She picked up a smelly rat under each arm and carried them in. Once in the kitchen, it was even more obvious that they not only smelt from their journey but also from the farm too.

They sat on the floor completely bemused. The little girl even shaking a bit. Well, let's get the horrid bit over first Joanna thought and went to fill the big kitchen sink with warm water. Fortunately, there were plenty of towels in the bathroom cupboard, so she ran upstairs to get them and some nice smelly shampoo. When she got back the pups hadn't moved. Boy was no problem, he even seemed to like the warm water and the massage as Joanna washed. She was soaked as she lifted him out and rubbed him as dry as she could. He then sat bemused. Where was Girl? She found her quivering under the table. And despite the fresh warm water, Girl managed to get each paw braced against a corner of the sink and struggled like mad. Each time Joanna removed one it went straight back. In the end, she lifted Girl up and released her quickly back in before the bracing could occur. There was a fight and a wriggle but at last, the job was done; the damp pup returned to her brother.

Joanna sniffed, hopefully, she wasn't nose blind. It was better smelling now. Utilising their quietness, she went to the back corridor and saw Ray was right. She found the old big soft dog bed, just the right size for one large labrador or two puppies; bowls, toys, even old collar and leashes. Perfect. She carried the bed into the sitting room and plonked the pups in it. They remained immobile, so she nipped out with newspapers and bucket and cleaned the Landrover; thanking heaven for the metal floor and old plastic seat. She returned with the food and old blanket and they were still there. Joanna dragged the basket and stinky rug into the sitting room and lit the fire. At the smell of the rug, the pups sniffed and re-animated. They twined around and grunted and sank into an exhausted sleep in the bed.

Joanna sighed, hopefully, the rug stink wouldn't be so strong. She took some pictures of them and posted them to the gang on Facebook. If only it would be always so easy thought Joanna, well aware that by next morning as they began to settle things might just change…

It began sooner than that. She had gone with the puppies into the garden when she went to bed, having found collars that fitted and the old leads. They'd leapt about with the new experience, but she couldn't risk losing two black dogs in a dark night. Putting a fence up was a priority; she didn't want to have to go out with them every night. They had both performed despite the landrover and having refused to eat and drink. She praised them, hopefully starting the right way. When they got back in, they finally snacked on the bowl of their food, had a drink, and got back into the basket. It certainly was too good to be true.

The whining from downstairs woke her at 4 am. Maybe this was milking time, and they were due out, she thought as she stumbled downstairs. Again, both pups performed and came happily back in. But they were now wide awake. She shut the door on them only for there to be a terrific crash before she got to the top of the stairs. When she looked in, the standard lamp was on the floor, its cable being chewed. Thankfully not plugged in.

There was no way she was staying awake, so she let them tackle their first stairs and come into her bedroom.

She collapsed under the quilt and listened to the pups investigating the room. Then they decided to jump on her. Being licked from two angles had her diving under which they just thought was a fantastic game. They jumped, leapt and snarled pretending to catch a mouse under the quilt. Then they ran around the room, knocking things over, but as quickly as they woke, they jumped back up on the bed. After more wriggling about they fell asleep.

It seemed too soon when the alarm went off at 7:30 and Joanna climbed bleary-eyed out of her bed. The pups thought this was fantastic and jumped about, tripping her over as she tried to dress. In desperation, she opened the bedroom door and let them downstairs. When she got down, she found they were tucking into their food. She would need to shop very, very soon. Naturally, her breakfast was much nicer, and she ate with two pairs of eyes boring into her. She discovered that she had two dribblers. That made her want to heave. She shouted 'Out' and pointed. To her surprise, they backed off and stayed there for a while. They even returned to their place on the mat when she noticed them creeping forward. Ha! Dog training was going to be easy!

# TEN

The next step was work. No more driving the half mile or so to the village; it was walkies now. She packed a rucksack with the blanket, food and some old dog toys and set off with the two on their improvised leads. This wasn't so easy as they both wanted to go in different directions or fought the lead. It was slow progress. But it was fun. The two started letting her into their world as she petted and encouraged them. Their enthusiasm for the bright morning was infective and Joanna arrived at the office with a big grin on her face.

'Hi girls, we've got two new members of staff!' And the two newcomers were greeted by the girls in the office with great glee. Dog lovers themselves, it was no hardship to play and cuddle the two. But work had to start. Joanna got the blanket and toys out and spread them in a gap between the desks. It worked for about five minutes. Then one needed out and then the other, then they disappeared under the cabinet and emptied the rubbish basket. Then Ray walked in. Joanna nearly laughed out loud as his face was a picture of horror.

'I didn't expect to find these two here,' he moaned.

'They'll be fine Dad, I've got their stuff here, and they'll settle it's all new to them.'

'Hmm, we'll see, they're on trial, especially if any customers come in,' he grudgingly said.

So, they did try, but it wasn't easy for anyone to concentrate. The two played and jumped and then discovered how to bark when the first visitor arrived. Ray got cross even though Joanna was doing her best to quieten them with distractions.

'For goodness sake, I can't hear myself speak. They're like double tornadoes. Take them outside or put them in the back room.' Joanna opted to take them outside and walk them around. She felt so despondent as she waited for the guy to go. There was no way they could do this every time they had people in; what was she going to do with them when she went to the Record office? Finally, she came in from the cold.

'I think those two are like a tornado that can't stop barking. I know, those two are just a pair of Barknadoes,' laughed Sheila catching Joanna's glum face. 'They'll be fine and misery guts has gone out on a visit.' It was easier for the rest of the day, but there had to be a better solution. Barknadoes seem to stick, although it quickly abbreviated to Nadoes. At lunchtime, they opened up the back room and tried to make it a dog room, but so much was stored in there; only a small space could be made. But at least they could be shut in there and the barking was muffled. There was the occasional accident when Joanna was so engrossed in her work and missed the warning signs. At last, it was home time. Joanna began her dreading thoughts when she imagined how it would be when they stepped up to full time in a few weeks. Still, now she was free to do some shopping. She had managed to buy a few doggy bits and pieces in the village shop as dogs were allowed in; but it needed a trip into town to get things. As she lurched home, she tried to work out the logistics. She needed a dog guard in her car, somewhere she could leave them when she went out. A garden fence; not to mention proper collars, leads, doggy gear and a visit to the vets. There was nothing for it, she would have to pad the car out with paper and cleaning stuff, put the seats down and drive very carefully. That was the priority.

Joanna shut the dogs in the house while she prepared the car; two concerned faces watching her through the glass back door. They weren't keen on the car either and went into silent mode as she lifted them in. They proceeded to glare as she drove the short distance, but happily only dribbled their disquiet. Unaware of dog tradition about hating vets they went in quite cheerfully. They snuffled and sniffed the strange smells, then went into full Barknado form when the Vet put his head around the door and beckoned them in. They soon quietened as a sympathetic and understanding hand allowed them to work it all out.

'Full injections, worming, chips?'

Joanna nodded.

'Right. Let's just check them over. How long have you had them?' Joanna explained, and the vet gave them a full clean bill of health; stuck needles in their unwitting necks, then asked if they would have little operations.

'Absolutely! When can we do this?' Joanna replied, anything to calm them down.

'In a couple of months. It will be better if we do them at the same time, so they won't be trying to get each other's stitches out. They'll be too concerned about themselves! Very brave you taking on two. I know their mother and she's extremely what should I say, active!' They laughed, and Joanna left the vets with two vaccinated and insured Barknadoes. Just the return visit for the repeat jab in a month and the little operations to plan.

Feeling like she was getting somewhere, she pulled in at the garage and ordered the brake for the back of the car. There was still just dribbling going on, so she dared to go further to the large pet store. To her surprise, she saw someone walk in with their dog, wow, dog-friendly! She got the two out, who thought it was another vets until they went through the door and sniffed the aroma of dog food, free samples and all sorts of dog treats. Joanna found someone to help her and spent a small fortune on everything dog. She had never realised there were so many things that they couldn't live without and she had double!

By the time she pulled into the yard, the dogs were getting whiny in the car and she guessed they needed a piddle break. Without thinking she let them out of the car and went towards the garden thinking they would follow. They both slithered out of the car and took off in full bark mode to where Diane was teaching a group of kids. Joanna ran as fast as she could but couldn't stop them tearing into the school and chasing the horses. One was startled and jumped about losing its rider and the others joined in. There was a lot of shrieking from the kids, but all Joanna could think of was catching the pups and getting them away. She yelled at them and for a split second she got their attention and grabbed one, but the other got away.

'Get those bloody animals out of my school!' yelled Diane, as she picked up the fallen rider. The others were all down at the end with one dog still barking at Diane. Joanna managed to catch the pup by the scruff of the neck and dragged her away. It wasn't easy trying to get the gate open and not lose them again. She slung them into the back of the car and ran back down to the school where things were calming down.

'I'm sorry Diane, it was just a slip. I'm ordering a fence, so they won't get out again.'

'Just typical of your selfishness Joanna. You never think of anyone but yourself. Sarah could have been hurt, I'll have to explain it all to her mother. Heavens knows what she'll say.'

'I'll speak to her myself and apologise. Look, I'm totally sorry, it won't happen again.'

'Too true it won't, if it does I'll have your dogs shot.'

This sent up a wail from Sarah who was next to her,

'No, don't kill the dogs, they're just babies!' This shut up Diane and Joanna made her escape. A car was pulling into the yard, so she beckoned to the driver.

'Are you Sarah's mum? Look, I'm really sorry, I've got two new puppies, and they scared the horses. Sarah fell off. She's not hurt though.'

'Oh, she bounces as she's always falling off anyway. Don't worry, it was just an accident I'm sure. What have you got?'

'Two pups from the Farm shop farm at Minchley.'

'That explains it, their mum is always legging it about the place. We live in the same village, don't worry.'

Diane arrived at this point. The ponies and kids were now in the yard untacking.

'Oh Mrs, Smith, I'm so sorry about this terrible incident. I'll make sure nothing like this happens again,' she glared at Joanna.

'Not a problem, we've got dogs too, don't think about it! Is Tuesday evening still okay for a lesson?'

'Oh, yes, but...of...course...' Deflated Diane nevertheless continued to glare at Joanna, so she made her escape.

Soon she had the unrepentant dogs in the house plus all their goodies and they were unpacking. Well, the pups were pulling the toys out of the wrappers when Ray walked in. Yet again a stony face.

'Joanna, I just heard about the dogs in the school.'

'Yes, I know Dad, I've apologised all round. I'm getting a fence organised as soon as possible.'

'That may take a while, so I've asked Jeff and Tony to come and put one up tomorrow. You'll have to pay their time because it's not estate work. However, the wood and wire will be free as it's old stuff from the showground.'

'Wow, thanks Dad that's really kind of you,' Joanna tried a big grin, not so long ago they would have had a brief, if a bit uncomfortable hug; but those days seemed long gone.

'Maybe it would have been better if you had waited as I said. I found this in my junk mail, it may help you.' He handed her a small flyer for puppy training classes in the next village and then went. Maybe he wasn't as cross as he looked. This was a great idea, she would be there on Friday.

The next couple of days were both exhausting and wonderful for Joanna. The team arrived early the next morning and put up a fence around all of her garden. They even brought a gate, so Joanna didn't have to go through the back door all the time and the dogs could go in and out as they wished from the sitting room. They loved the garden and played together mad puppy games, with mock fighting and puppy races zigzagging like coursing greyhounds. They soon found a favourite place under an old lavender bush and Joanna soon found that if it was too quiet, more than likely they were asleep in the hole they'd dug there.

House training wasn't always successful, neither needed a pee at the same time. While they were quick to learn, sometimes Joanna guessed she missed the prompts. Their appetites grew daily. They were bottomless pits, but her gut feeling was not to let them feed at will but rather three small meals a day where she could control what was eaten. Boy was always inclined to steal from Girl as she was a relatively slower eater. What was best was their friendship; the riotous greetings, that they loved her, even if it was for the food, and she gave up with them sleeping downstairs. If they were on the bed, she knew if they needed out in the night. She was thankful for her double bed because two medium-sized pups, when stretched out, took up a lot of room. She rang Gloria and told her about the dogs and their adventures. She shrieked with laughter about the horse chasing. She'd helped Joanna's woes after Christmas and was always at the end of the phone. As soon as Joanna had time, and they travelled better, she had to take them to see her.

The office was not much better where they had to bark at all newcomers, but Ray hadn't been around too much. When he was she had kept a firmer eye on things. Friday morning and no work was a great relief. Bleary-eyed, she let them out into the warm sunshine, which started another joyous romp around the garden. Coffee was what she needed now. As the kettle boiled, there was a tap on the door and Chloe came in. Joanna was engulfed in the usual warm embrace which was thankfully brief. She hadn't seen much of Chloe recently and still felt betrayed by her lack of support when before Christmas they'd seemed to be becoming such close friends.

'So where are your two babies?'

At the sound of a new voice, the Barknadoes came tearing in at full volume. Chloe got down on her knees and in seconds they were all over her, slobbering and telling her she was their new best friend.

'Heartless things aren't they?' exclaimed Joanna. 'Complete tarts!'

'Oh, they know when someone loves them. I'd love another dog but I'm not settled enough yet,' said Chloe through puppy. 'Have they got names yet?'

'No, they get called collectively the Barknadoes and I can't think of names that I can shout,' laughed Joanna.

Chloe finally stood up with the two still bouncing about.

'Do I smell coffee?'

'You do.' Joanna relaxed and filled two mugs.

'How are they settling in? I hear they've had a few adventures.'

Joanna grimaced, 'That's all sorted now that I've got a fence and tonight we're off to puppy school. Then maybe they'll be quieter at work. It's early days yet.'

'That's great, oh, I do envy you them. Do they sleep on your bed?'

'But of course!' They laughed and had a long dog talk over their coffees. Joanna began to forgive Chloe, who was very caught up in the wedding stuff and was clearly itching to talk about it, but Joanna veered off the subject; especially as she was no longer Maid of Honour. Finally, Chloe looked at her watch, 'I must dash, we've got a dress fitting. Are you still certain you won't?'

'No Chloe, I don't think that Diane and I are friends any more and it wouldn't be right.'

Chloe sighed,' Ah well, maybe God has his hand on all this. If you ever need help with these two, let me know. I'd love to be a dog sitter. I'd get some wedding stress therapy from them.' She was looking at the pups who were tumbling around trying to destroy a plastic bone.

'Maybe you could if you're not too busy. I need to start my work at the Record office, so I can run our archive. Harry said I need about six weeks. If you could look after them on the days I go? They can't be left on their own for any length of time yet.'

'Oh, that sounds wonderful, yes please, when do you go?'

'Next Wednesday?'

Chloe took her phone from her pocket and scrolled through.

'Yup can do. I'll be round first thing to collect them or you can drop them off. But it'll cost you.'

Joanna took a mental step back.

'I've just thought of good names that suit them!'

'Go on.'

'Jack and Jill. That's just how they rush and tumble around the place, but no vinegar and brown paper!'

And the names stuck.

# ELEVEN

It was with some trepidation that Joanna got the dogs out of the car, wiped off the dribble and went into the hall. She hated going into new places; she didn't know anyone and wanted to forget the whole thing and go home. Inside there were about six dogs and their owners who were chatting to of all people, Security man. It was as if they had never danced at Christmas, Joanna felt paralysed. He saw her and came over. It seemed he was in charge.

'Well fancy meeting you again,' he almost smiled. 'And who are these two?'

'Jack and Jill. I know, crazy names but they seem to like them.'

'And what can I do for you?'

'Well, we need some training, not only just growing up stuff, and they are rather good at barking.'

'And how old are they, are they fully vaccinated?'

'About four months and they had their first jab a couple of days ago.'

'Well, I'm sorry on a number of counts. They must have had the top up one too, and I need to see the certificates. This is a ten-week course and we're halfway through; it wouldn't help you or the others if you join now.'

Joanna's spirits fell. She'd had such hopes that she could get the pups sorted and she could start doing things with them.

'There is a solution. I offer home training as well if there are some issues you need help with. With such a young pair we can get a good start on this barking!' he now smiled, and it changed his face; far less grumpy.

'That would be amazing! Yes, I have a lot of questions and things I know I must do better, when can you come?'

'Are you sure, my fees may be very high?'

'I'm sure it'll be worth every penny.'

'OK, here's my card. Ring me later this evening, about Nine and we can arrange a date. I must dash now as they're all agog watching us, speak later.' He turned to his class, who Joanna noticed seemed to be glaring at her; most interesting.

Joanna had trouble convincing the pair that they shouldn't meet their new friends, and they made their way home. She took the time to check Mr Security man out as he had a web address on the card. Guy had worked with several of the most famous dog trainers but was now making his own schemes and courses. Everything was based on kindness and positive reinforcement. He had schools in several of the local towns and there were great testimonies from satisfied customers. There was a little biography too, he had a degree in history, majoring in the Victorian era. Same age as her and single. Maybe her first impressions of the fat, ginger security man had been wrong; he was certainly slimmer these days. Joanna sniggered to herself and picked up the phone.

The weekend flew past with playing with the dogs and chilling. The only down point was the damage done when she went out. It was as if some retributive frenzy took over them and anything of hers was game. She lost several shoes, books and some china ornaments got knocked to the ground and smashed. She gritted her teeth and hoped her saviour would have some remedies. They were bad at work on Monday too, even the girls in the office were a bit exasperated, so Joanna packed up her work and took it home.

The afternoon couldn't come too quickly, and she was so relieved when Guy turned up promptly. She had decided to let him see them at their worst so did nothing to stop the leaping and barking at the doorbell. To her surprise, he did nothing but just came in and sat down at the kitchen table and let the pups calm down. Which happened, and they lost interest in him and mooched out into the garden.

'Right, now I can see the problem, but it's not unsolvable. I was looking at the body language and its just pure excitement, they're friendly and they have no issues. First of all, we will encourage them to speak. Can you call them back in?' he said briskly.

Joanna did, and the pandemonium returned. This time Guy encouraged them saying, 'speak' and waving his hand at them, keeping eye contact, which he pointed out. As soon as they quieted, which wasn't too long as they'd already met him, he said, 'Quiet' and to their joy produced a snack. He reinforced this two or three times, then made Joanna do it. To her amazement, they did it for her too. They then worked for about fifteen minutes going between 'quiet 'and 'speak'.

'Now let them play in the garden. They've learnt a lot. Bet you think they're cleverer than you thought!'

'That's amazing, so now when someone comes in the office, if I say quiet, they should be so, especially if there's a snack involved?'

'You got it, but you will need to work at them and not relax about it. What next?'

'The destruction derby when I go out?'

'Where do you leave them?'

'Well in the house. I can't leave them in the garden as they'll bark at the horses. They've already chased them once...'

'We'll put horse aversion therapy on the list, 'he grinned. 'Do you have a room or a corner you could make for them, removing all dangerous objects?'

'Not really. I don't like this caging of dogs at all, something just says it's wrong.'

Then Joanna had an idea. 'There is the old gun room down the corridor that I could use; shall we look?' Indeed, the gun room was perfect if full of junk, but it had a window and was light. In fact, despite the old cupboards, there was plenty of room for two growing dogs.

'What do you think?'

'This is ideal, but you mustn't make it into a prison. There should be happy associations with it'.

'You mean food and toys?'

'Exactly. Plenty of comfortable things to lie on that are allowed to be destroyed. These two are food orientated, that helps.' Joanna burst out laughing but he continued. 'Toys that take their time, such as toys which trickle snacks out, there's a wealth of them to try. Then put them in there at first with the toys for a few minutes, but not necessarily that the toys are emptied out. And the toys must only found here, despite the fact that they will want to steal them. They will soon find it a place they like to go, do short trips at first. Then over the months you can extend the time, but never more than one or two hours and load the toys accordingly. Make it a place they associate with food and fun. As they grow they will chew less and less, then you'll be able to relax the food loadings.' Joanna wasn't so sure about that but passed it by, his calm a reasonable way was giving her hope.

'Wow, that's so simple, and I never thought of it.'

'Right now, we need to do some more quiet and speak and discuss a training plan for you, and in a few weeks, you can join the classes. You can use the same principles to sit and stay, but don't overdo it, make it fun and keep the rewards going. They need to socialise, so if you have some doggy friends, meet up with them so they can play, as long as their dogs are fully vaccinated. I have to be careful in the school with regulations and so on…'

As they went back to the kitchen and sat at the table to sign the papers that Guy had brought about his fees and conditions, the Barknadoes returned in full volume. Joanna held her hand up and said 'quiet', looking at them, it worked. She was bowled over and gave them more snacks and even felt like hugging Guy but resisted the idea.

'What will be our plan over the coming weeks?' she asked as he made to leave, he seemed to have forgotten this bit. He sat down again.

'I think with these two, we'll have to do doorbell work using quiet, greeting people quietly, which will be difficult for them as they are people lovers; but I think those are their main issues. Try taking them to nice places in the car, I'm sure it'll help stop the drooling. It's a growing up thing. It'll then be lead training, oh, and horse training. They are nice genuine dogs, don't walk them too much, puppies need to play. Do exercise them on a couple, it'll be much easier!'

The Barknadoes turned on the charm for Guy playing with much gusto and fake growling. He paused to watch them.

'How long have you been training?' asked Joanna trying to find something other than dogs to talk about.

'Two years with my business, but on and off for a long time. I've turned my hand to many things in the meantime to make ends meet.'

They both laughed, and Guy again rose from the chair almost as if he didn't want to continue the conversation. 'Same time next week?'

'That would be great.'

And he was gone. Joanna turned to the dogs who were looking sadly at the closed door. 'Never mind, he'll be back next week. Let's make you a doggy heaven.' Maybe she felt sad too.

The afternoon flew past as Joanna cleared the gun room of all the extra junk. She even found her treasure box again and put that aside to rummage through later. Most of the junk she had absolutely no idea why it was kept, so she chucked the lot. Then it was old blankets for sleeping on, lots of them to tear and chew. The floor was lino so cleaning would be oaky.

Then it was on the internet to order lots of new time-consuming toys. Joanna found there were bacon flavoured bubble machines and even ball chucking toys that the dogs could learn to retrieve and fill themselves; these could wait. Joanna felt confident for the first time in a long while as the dogs played and got under her feet; now it was fun.

That evening, she let the dogs run in and out of their new room then shut it and settled down to look through her diaries. Why had she stopped writing at Mia's death? She would have liked to touch base with all her emotions, especially after she gave up on the horses. It was as good as a pony book when she read about her meeting the older Diane and how they had hit it off. But what surprised her was her anger at her mother. The moaning about not being allowed to go to the local youth club and parties, all because the horses had to come first. She remembered the strength of her mother again. Joanna might have been a pony loving kid, but her mother was pushing her so hard that the love of horses was almost being beaten out of her. She'd never realised this, so maybe the rebellion would have happened at some stage if her mother had lived. It was a huge shock which had her gazing blankly at the TV and not seeing the dogs destroying her favourite cushion for quite some time.

However, the next morning it all took a new perspective, it was the past. She took lots of treats to work and amazed the office girls on the progress. They also made the back room another dog proof, happy place, so the dogs wouldn't feel it was a punishment room. Even Ray was impressed with the new training and had to take the credit for having found the trainer; but he wasn't in the office long.

Even the girls had noticed how little time he was around and made smutty jokes about young love thinking

Joanna didn't hear. The whole village seemed to know about the upcoming nuptials and it was a great source of speculation. Joanna tried her best, saying that she had little to do with it but was happy for her dad.

Some of the boxes in the back room were full of old records of the show, reaching back to the 1890s when it had started. These Joanna took home to put in the archive room. That had all gone quiet until her training was done, and the link was put up, but the training started the next day. She was excited about something else new and for herself alone.

Joanna took the dogs and a box of goodies to Chloe's early the next morning. Chloe answered the door a bit bleary-eyed but perked up at the sight of the Nadoes. They rushed in to check out her toys and snacks. Joanna showed her the new training and felt sure Chloe would be fine. As she reminded her about letting them out, Chloe vanished talking to the dogs about what fun they were all going to have. Joanna made her escape.

# TWELVE

Joanna didn't feel so confident as she stood outside the Record office. It was a big modern, angular building which she found quite overwhelming. Yet in she went finding Harry waiting for her. He was bubbling with enthusiasm and began giving her more information than she could take in as her ID was taken, she got a label and was signed in. Firstly, she was given a tour of all the departments, from documents to photos to sound. Most interesting was the arrivals, where things gifted were checked over and a basic catalogue entry made.

'It must be like Christmas here when you get lots of exciting things turning up!' she exclaimed.

'We have had some great finds, but some of it is very run of the mill, boxes of old newspapers, bills and birthday cards. The trouble is we can't keep everything as much as we'd like to.'

'But surely everything has some merit and may have an importance we don't see now?'

'We just can't physically do it. Some things we return with suggestions to the families, that helps. I don't like it either. But we can't keep loads of bills and things, we sometimes just take a selection.'

'So, we've done you a favour keeping ours?'

'Yes, in a way, but we would have loved to have got our hands on some of your stuff!' He smirked a big grin and Joanna laughed which got a stern look from one of the staff.

'It's worse than a library!'

'Yes, we're a quiet lot, let's look at the main reading room.'

The main room was also encased in a hush, with many big tables for reading with special lecterns for big books. They spent the next couple of hours going through the whole process of reading the databases and microfiches, ordering the documents, handling them the returning them. Then Harry gave Joanna her first job.

'Just to refresh your mind about the document process, ask at the desk for a parcel in your name. You'll receive a bundle of Marriage certificates from the 16 and 17th century. Very often the only person in the village who could read or write was the Blacksmith. You will find most couples have signed with crosses. But I need you to simply order them alphabetically under the groom's name for each year. There's a lot of them, so that'll keep you quiet today. At lunchtime we'll nip over to the café,' and he left her adrift.

She collected the brown documents and spent a few minutes familiarising herself with the language and just seeping into the unwritten history behind them all. Even the feel of the paper was exciting and romantic. She was thoroughly immersed until lunchtime, but she also took in the aura of the rooms; the people searching intensively for long lost family, the scribbling on notes and laptops, excitement when someone was found. She found it fascinating and just loved it. At lunchtime, Harry whisked her to the café where they feasted on burgers and chips and Joanna told Harry about the puppies. From there the conversation went in all directions. Away from documents, Harry had an opinion on everything which was sometimes daft or funny.

The time flew past as he held most of the conversation which Joanna found both restful and irritating when she couldn't get her own comment in. Too soon they returned to the office and more certificates; Harry saying he'd see her the same time the following week. Later that afternoon, Joanna drove home, reflecting on her day. She came to the conclusion that it was one of the best she'd had for ages. She loved the scholarly intense atmosphere too; she couldn't wait for her next trip.

At Chloe's, the dogs greeted her in their best tornado manner, nearly knocking her over, training completely forgotten. Joanna was so pleased to see them, she naughtily let it go. Chloe told her all about their adventures and the misadventure in the dustbin, but she was more than happy for next week. She touched on the wedding to say that after all, it was going to be in the local church and the reception at the pub; they just hadn't been able to find anything better.

'Are you still resolute that you won't be the Maid of Honour?'

'Chloe, as I've said, we're not on speaking terms, they stay in their side and me in mine. Dad never pops in anymore, he spends the minimum time in the office and I don't like to go in. I can't see a resolution.'

'Well that's such a shame, yet I will not butt in between you all. I can see both sides and don't want to get caught in the flack. I had that enough with one of Diane's affairs. May can seem a long time away, but time is flying.' Chloe looked thoughtful. 'anyway, I'm going to love having the dogs if nothing else. See you next week.'

Time did tick on quickly. Over the next weeks, as winter turned into spring, the puppies grew in stature if not in good behaviour. Guy came each week for lessons sometimes they were perfect, sometimes not so. He was always polite and formal, and Joanna found it a bit frustrating that he wasn't friendlier. It was as if he was playing a trainer's role and hiding behind it. She tried her best to crack this shell, but he wouldn't be drawn. Maybe it was this challenge that found Joanna thinking of Guy in odd moments of the day…

Jack and Jill met new friends on walks around the village. On the couple they worked as a team and even the pulling got better. Joanne realised that some of this was her speeding up to meet them! They loved going to visit Chloe and even more so Gloria whose two Labradors became their best pals. The Barknadoes were so alike in character they could have been interchangeable. Like twins, they acted badly and well in unison. After Easter Joanna finally joined the new class at puppy school. To her surprise, Guy took one pup from her every week leaving her to concentrate on one. It was fun, learning simple control, and they came into their own over the small obstacle course he put up. Joanna was amazed at how Guy changed in the new setting. He was far more friendly with the group of mostly women and they seemed to like him. Joanna noted how a few of the women were rather well made up and in best clothes rather than her own doggy gear. That caused an inner chuckle, how shameless!

Joanna didn't hit it off with the group despite them all being new to the course. Offers of meeting for walks or coffee seemed to fall on deaf ears. She could only put it down to them feeling she was a favourite of Guy's because of the home training and that he took her dogs, not theirs. He showed little favouritism to her, if anything he was harder on her performance than the others. It kept Joanna amused trying to figure him out.

The pups had their little operations, a bit early for Joanna's liking but the vet was of the opinion they were ready; so she was nursemaid for two sore dogs. They soon recovered and became almost different characters. Still playful, but calmer and more loving; easier to walk out and they now came back more when called. Guy had caught her shouting at them when they returned after they had been doing some outdoor training and they had gone hunting for rabbits. He pointed out the illogicality of it, and so Joanna rewarded all but the worst adventures with treats. The result was the two now wanted to be with her more than ever. Both had shot up and were near Labrador size, if not quite so wide.

The show season was warming up, and Sheila was being given more and more of Ray's work to do; she wasn't happy with the load. Joanna spent more time in the office to help, thankful that the Barknadoes were now full team members and sometimes now would even sleep through visitors coming in. Ray and Diane were around but Joanna noticed that they often took off for days at a time and the riding school wasn't at all busy. The ponies and Challenger were becoming fat with lack of work as the spring grass came through.

The Record Office was the highlight of her week and she learnt about the office systems, how to handle fragile documents, add things to the database and how to order new collections. She even helped people with their enquiries as she became familiar with all the different sources. She became used to wearing the thin gloves to protect documents and ordered some for home. Though she loved the work, she felt a sense of inadequacy when she didn't know the historical context and events around the documents. She began to read around the subject to build background knowledge.

Lunch with Harry was always a giggle and infuriating as they chatted about the world. They laughed at how some of the visitors were sometimes so intense, that they even ascribed characters to long-dead people who they would never meet. She had even half hoped that Harry might ask her for a date, but it never happened. On Valentine's day her post box was as empty as ever. It didn't help when she saw a bouquet being delivered to the main front door.

At the end of April, Harry pronounced her ready to begin running the house archive and so it was planned to put it online after the wedding. Harry would come over to check it was all okay, and he was going to look over her cataloguing of the show material. Joanna had found the very local history fascinating and wanted to add it all to the database.

The beginning of May was warm and seemed almost an enchanted month; greener than ever as Joanna took the dogs on walks around the valley where she used to ride; now enjoying the dogs' madcap adventures. Despite her lack of involvement, she picked up the marriage excitement from Chloe when they took the dogs for walks together. She tried her best not to flood her with stuff, apologising each time. Diane, Joanna managed to avoid by never going through the baize door and keeping away from the stables; she didn't bother to watch the therapy, she was too busy.

She kept hold of her happiness for Ray but there was never the opportunity to talk, even at work. She couldn't pinpoint where she reached this, but it was just a feeling that it was right that he had a love and was happy again; even if the love wasn't the best one in her opinion. In some ways, Joanna felt bereaved but knew she had to get on with her life without her dad's close presence. She made the best she could of adjusting. She had her wedding invitation; the big day was now May the 28th. She had wondered if she would get one, so at least she could enjoy some shopping for a new outfit.

Then one afternoon, shortly before the big day Chloe popped in and for once looked nervous, which was maybe because she had Diane and Ray behind her. The dogs behaved perfectly and even took themselves to their beds. Joanna heaved an inward sigh of relief.

'Now, please no arguments, I have something I want to tell you all. Now as you know, I've been wanting to go back to Wales, and I've found a lovely cottage near the church I used to go to and I will move back after the wedding.' All murmured their congratulations but still felt apprehensive.

'Now, I've been thinking about my wedding gift and I have something for you all. Now I know there have been disagreements and misunderstandings – don't forget I get it from all sides being in the middle as it were. The relationships between all three of you cannot continue like this. It must be sorted.' All had the grace to hang their heads to the ground, avoiding eye contact.

'So, this weekend, you are all off to Wales yourselves for some therapy work. It's in a neutral, loving environment, where you can work together to sort this all out. It's all paid for; the accommodation is five star. Only thing is, you will have to have single rooms, its part of the ethos of the place.'

'Oh no Mum, not Ethan and Sue?' wailed Diane

'But where else? They have the most brilliant results; they are both qualified therapists.' Chloe replied firmly.

'What she hasn't said is that they're equine therapy. And Christians. Oh, couldn't we do this another way?' wailed Diane.

'No Diane, do this for me. I want to settle back in Wales knowing you're all happy. Please.'

'Well, it can't do any harm I suppose,' said Ray warily. 'Things haven't been as I imagined they would be.' He stared purposefully at Joanna.

'I'm up for it,' said Joanna, just to be bloody-minded. 'I guess you'll look after the dogs and the horses Chloe?'

She nodded, 'I've already got back up sorted if there are any problems.'

'If they're going, I guess I have to go,' grudged Diane at last.

'Great! Fantastic!' Chloe glowed and tried to hug them all.

On Friday morning, in two cars because Joanna refused to share, with a group sense of dread, the three took off for Wales.

# THIRTEEN

Joanna arrived first having quickly left the other car behind on the motorway. She was bowled over by the Eighteenth century manor house and stood for a couple of minutes just drinking it in through her newly emerging sense of history. Cherry trees were in bloom all around; it looked like something from a calendar. She made her way through the huge stone entrance and was surprised at how light the hall was. A lot of battle flags and dead animals festooned the walls, but the seating was modern, and it looked smart.

'Hello, you must be Joanna!' A middle-aged woman appeared from behind the desk.' I'm Sue, and I just want to welcome you here to our house with love, and an invitation to leave all your cares here.'

Hippie thought Joanna.

'I'll show you to your room, and then supper will be at seven. We are also a small hotel as well as a therapy centre, but it's quiet this time of year, so we have the place to ourselves. This weekend, we'll have our meals in the kitchen.'

'That's fine with me,' managed Joanna. She followed Sue up a circular staircase and was ushered into a room with a view over a large country park.

'Wow, that's quite a garden!' exclaimed Joanna.

'Yeah, it's a swine to mow!' laughed Sue. Joanna began to warm to her. She was shown an en-suite with a bath; there was a welcome tray with a kettle and best of all large four-poster bed. Joanna laughed as she took it in.

'I'm so glad I don't have the dogs with me, I'd be on the floor.'

Sue laughed too, and they then had a very cosy dog talk.

'Right, now settle yourself in. If you'd like a swim or a sauna, they're at the back of the house. There's a box of old cossies if you haven't one. But most of all, could you spend a little time on this form for me? Just give me your opinion of why you're here, a bit of background, it helps us to help you.'

With a smile, Sue was gone. Joanna took the form and frowned, the questions were apparently simple, but so much needed to be said. What could she do but give an honest version of the events of the past few months? She found a pen, made a coffee and settled down to write.

It seemed to take forever, and Joanna was glad to finish and make her way down to reception. This time a man was sat there, who introduced himself as Ethan. He was tall thin and very bald. More hippie thought Joanna again as she handed her work over.

'The others arrived not long after you and are doing their forms. Would you like some tea or coffee and we can all meet up in the main hall?'

'I'd just like to have a look around the house, Sue said there's no other guests? We live in a Victorian house but not quite the same. History is my new interest.'

'Be my guest, only place off limits is through the baize door into the servants' quarters which is our flat.'

'Funny, I live through a baize door too!'

'You're the family slave then?'

'No, I moved into our servants' wing as I needed some space when I was at college and never went back.'

Joanna wandered around the house and looking in the bedrooms, ducking away from the two that had no key hanging out. The pool and sauna were new additions, but what she liked was the reception rooms, furnished in period furniture with pictures of the family who had lived there; and best was the library. Her newly honed archivists' senses saw lots of old estate documents in a case and fragile books just jammed on the shelves that looked too old to be touched without gloves. How she itched to rummage through. Then she heard someone calling her name and made her way back to reception. Diane and Ray were just handing over their stuff, looking sheepish at the sight of Joanna.

'Great, we're all together!' Sue appeared with what seemed to be her ever-present grin.' Let's all sit here, I've put some goodies on the table and I'll explain everything. This is my family home and we run it as a therapy, Christian retreat and Conference centre besides being just a hotel. Ethan and I are trained counsellors and equine assisted therapy facilitators. We've run the centre for ten years, and so we have a wide experience in the field.

Now, while we are both active Christians, this is not the time or place to share our faith with you, and it will not be a part of the work we will do with you this weekend. However, if you have questions we will answer to the best of our ability. On Sunday morning we have a service in our chapel which you are welcome to attend.

We will begin our work with you in the next few minutes as we'll take a stroll down to the field and have a look at our horses. They are our partners in all this and have an equal say in what and how we do things. In the next two days we will meet in the indoor school, and in there do different exercises with the horses. Through your interaction, or not, we will then later chat about the session in a relaxed, non-threatening manner and see if we can help with any issues that come up. All we ask of you is complete honesty and you are free to express any emotion you need to. We take care of your safety with the horses.

Diane, we both know you are trained in this therapy, but from the courses we've all attended, you'll know being on the other side of the fence as it were, and despite any amount of practice, it can be extremely powerful for you. I hope you will be with us with an open mind. Likewise, Joanna, you have experience with horses, but I think this may be something completely new for you! Ray, you might have your socks blown off! Let's meet the horses.'

Still avoiding talking to each other, they made their way out past the stables at the back of the house. In a small field were five horses mooching about as there was little grass. Sue and Ethan took the lead and in the manner of horse watchers, leant on the fence.

'Have a look at the horses and tell us something about them.'

'They're watching and assessing us, watch out,' hissed Diane to Joanna who jumped as this was the first time she had spoken to her in ages. There was a pause and Ray spoke up,

'They all look pretty bored as there's nothing to eat.'

'Must they have something to eat?' asked Ethan.

'Well, that's what they do best, isn't it? Stuffing their faces all the time.'

'Is that your experience with them then?'

'Yea, like kids, always hungry and wanting something.'

Joanna felt herself tensing up, did he mean her?

'If these horses were you, which one is most like you?' interjected Sue, changing the focus. There was a pause.

'I guess that chestnut one is like me,' said Joanna.
'Why?'

'Well apart from having the same blonde hair colour in the mane, it's found a bit of paper and is mouthing it! I'm looking after the family records and I've been having training at the Records office. If I see a bit of old paper now, I have to check it out!'

They all laughed.

'I guess you've been in the library then!' snorted Ethan. 'Diane, what about you?'

'Oh heck, I know how much my answer is loaded. OK, If I have to make a choice, I like the big bay.'

'Why?'

'Can't put my finger on it. He's the best-looking horse of the group. I can't think of any other reason.'

Just at that moment, the bay decided to annoy all the others; bustling into the group who had all settled into dozing.

'OMG! That's so freaky, did he hear me? That's what I used to do to Dad when I was a kid if he was asleep on the sofa I just couldn't resist waking him up!' yelped Diane.

'How did he react?'

'Sometimes he was shamming, but sometimes he'd leap up like he was terrified come to think of it. I suppose it was his military training.'

'Did he ever scare you?'

'No never, he was always in control of himself and we'd have a cuddle and laugh.'

'You did that to me the other day,' said Ray. 'Why?'

'I all of a sudden felt I had to. Let me think about this,' said Diane looking at the ground.

'Well Ray, have you a favourite yet?' butted in Sue.

'Oh, easy for me, it's that grey one. Always Mia's favourite colour, we nearly bought one instead of Challenger, but we were beaten to the post. Can't think of any other reason either,' He smiled at Joanna for the first time in months. There was a pause and quietness as each was allowed their own thoughts.

'Well, I guess enough is enough, let's eat!'

They were led into what was the original kitchen with a huge but modern range, a farmhouse table and a feast laid out by the cook, who was introduced as Ruby.

They had onion soup, roast beef and apple crumble. The conversation was general, mostly lead by Sue and Ethan as the three still weren't yet able to even begin a three-way conversation or even any sort of conversation. Joanna suddenly felt exhausted even though it was only nine and went to bed. It was nice to sprawl on the bed without dogs, and she wondered if they were with Chloe in her bedroom. She felt apprehensive about the morning to come. In this new setting, the barriers between them all seemed all the stronger and now she acknowledged she'd been part of their being built. How they could be torn down she had no idea but maybe that wasn't her job. With that thought, she fell asleep.

# FOURTEEN

After the big meal in the evening, Joanna didn't expect to want breakfast the next morning, but the smell of cooking bacon and not having to share it with two hungry monsters was too appealing. She was first in the kitchen, and Ruby greeted her with a warm smile. Soon Diane and Ray arrived and with a non-committal, 'Morning,' they too ate well.

'What time do we have to be at the school?' asked Joanna.

'In about half an hour. Did you sleep well?' answered Ray.

'Like a log without having to share the bed with the dogs!'

'But you don't have to share,' snapped Diane.

'It's my choice, what's that to you?'

'Well don't moan about it then.'

'I wasn't. I was just saying how pleasant it was for once, I'll be missing them tonight I expect.'

Joanna couldn't believe Diane's attitude, so she got up from the table and made her way down to the yard. It was a pleasant place with flower tubs and fresh blue paint on the doors. Joanna felt she had landed in one of the magical pony land places from her childhood dreams. She mooched about, looking in the stables, which were mostly empty. She wandered over to the school and found Sue and Ethan waiting. Four horses were in there, the three they had liked the previous night and a shetland.

'Morning! You look fresh and ready for action!' smiled Ethan.

'Yup, I guess the other two are on their way. Your stable yard is beautiful, like a dream from a pony book!'

'But I saw some of Chloe's pictures of yours, that's not bad,' said Sue

'Yeah, I suppose so, I guess you don't appreciate what's on your doorstep.'

'That's very profound!' The two laughed and just at that moment Ray and Diane came in. Joanna couldn't help noticing the nasty look Diane gave her.

'Right now! Welcome to your first session. You will each be given a task to do with the horses. Afterwards, when you consider it is completed, we'll have a discussion with you individually. Then when all have done, we'll have a break to reflect, then coffee. We ask you not to comment to each other during it or give instructions. Let the person go through it in their own way. Right. Each one of you will have the same task this time, which is bring us a horse. We'll sit here behind this rope and we won't cross it. We might say something if we feel there's a need, but we'll just take it quietly and slowly. Any questions? No? Right. Off you go then Ray, bring a horse to us by any means you feel you can use.'

Ray crossed over the rope and approached the horses cautiously. When he got near, the shetland came up and began sniffing him. He shoved it away and made his way to the grey horse he had liked. The shetland was still following. Ray went up to the grey who sniffed him, and he gently took the forelock and tried to lead the horse. It wouldn't move. He spoke to it and tugged it again. On the third time, it moved and came docilely with Ray over to the others with the shetland following. He stopped at the rope.

'I'm finished,' he said.

'OK,' said Ethan.' How was that for you?'

'Well, I thought at first the horse wasn't going to move. I did a bit with the horses when my wife was alive and remembered pulling their manes, seeing as there are no halters around. Oh! The blighter!' Ray jumped and turned around as the shetland was biting his coat. 'Shoo, I don't want you!'

The others couldn't help laughing.

'Looking at this task, what are your thoughts?'

'Well, it's silly. It annoyed me when the horse wouldn't move and this little thing even more.'

'We'll be talking about metaphors a lot this weekend, and you're all here to sort some things out. Take this away with you. Is this in any way a metaphor, or a likeness, or a pattern that continues in your life?'

Ray, looking thoughtful sat down.

'Joanna, please collect a horse for us.'

With great trepidation, because she didn't like all those eyes on her, Joanna made her way into the arena. She had considered that it would be easy just to talk to the Shetland, but that was no challenge. She, instead, went for the big bay that Diane had liked. She walked up to him, casually with her hands in her pockets, the shetland following her too, so she ignored him. She reached the horse and talked to him gently, clicked, said, 'come' and he followed her straight back to the rope.

'I'm finished.' She kept an eye out for the shetland.

'How was that for you?'

'It took me back to when I had ponies as a kid and how sometimes it was just nice to be with them and walk with them. Challenger used to follow me everywhere...' Joanna to her surprise found herself welling up. 'Now he hates me, every time I go near him, he tries to bite or kick me, and I don't know why.'

Diane began to say something, but Sue shushed her with her hand.

'Can you tell us anything about your choice of horse?'

Joanna thought for a moment. Then grinned. 'Maybe I was subconsciously treading on someone's territory,' but she kept her eyes away from Diane.

'Just hold on to that until afterwards Joanna; and we'll discuss it.'

'Now, last but not least, Diane, please collect us a horse!'

Diane marched into the arena, once again dogged by the shetland. She turned around and gave it a huge shove each time it got near, even growling at it too. Finally, it sloped off. Now Diane took herself to the big bay, gave it a slap on the shoulder, then spoke to it firmly. Nothing. Each time she did it more firmly. Nothing. In fact, if anything, it backed onto her. She was getting angry, and the horse more bolshy.

'Diane, what do you think is happening here. Come over a little closer,' called Sue. Diane came over, 'stupid animal is just bolshy, he should know who is in command. With or without a headcollar.'

'OK, are you going to continue?'

'I haven't achieved my goal, you interrupted, so yes.' She marched back to the horse and this time slapped it on the rump. No reaction. The shetland was still behind her, so she turned around. 'Come on then, you're not going to let me down!' And the shetland marched briskly back to the rope with her.

'I'm finished!' she said glaring at the shetland.

'Do you feel you have completed the task?'

'No.'

'Do you want to have another go?'

'No, I've had enough of this. 'Diane marched off out of the school.

'Right you all now need to take a break. Leave Diane to sort herself out, please. If you go out through the yard, you can get into the gardens, where there are loads of seats. We'd like you not to talk to each other, but to reflect on all this and be back in half an hour when the coffee and cakes will have arrived.'

Joanna took off, as she needed to think. She soon found herself in a walled garden and sank onto an old bench. Everything whirled around in her mind. Mostly she was overwhelmed by how she had enjoyed the contact with the horse, the feeling of sympathy, friendliness and wanting to be with her. So far removed from the hard work and discipline that was around the horses and her mum. Could it be that she was wrong about herself becoming a pot hunting maniac? That if she had gone on, she would have found a quieter and happier place with the horses? For the first time in ages, she wanted to talk to Diane as she had been there. Not her dad, as he had always been distanced from the horses as even then he was running the show, but he had been there. Joanna heaved a huge sigh and headed back to the yard.

She was the last back but smiled at the other two as she grabbed a mug of coffee. Diane seemed to have retained some good humour.

'How was that for you?' asked Ray.

'Bit overpowering! I can see how this therapy works so well. I wonder what we'll have to do next?'

'If my guess is right, grooming and chatting,' said Diane unexpectedly.

'Was this where you trained before?'

'No, so at least I don't know the horses and their techniques so well!'

Sue and Ethan came into the yard with the three horses and tied them up in the sun.

'All done with coffee? Right, we'd like you to groom the horses and we'll chat together as you do it.'

'Told you!' grinned Diane for once.

All three found a box of grooming equipment by their horse and got stuck in. Joanna regained the smooth swing she had learnt in childhood and became absorbed in the movement, smells and contact.

'Tell us what you're thinking,' asked Sue. Joanna jumped as she was so immersed in the work.

'I'm beginning to think that maybe my giving up horses and riding wasn't such a good decision. But not that I'd want to go back to competing. I think I would still be highly competitive and then I'd lose what I'm enjoying now.'

'What's that?'

'The contact, smell and touching of the horse. Feeling a relationship with him. The first exercise made it clear. My mum was really into competing but didn't make it into the top rank. She gave it up when she got married. I guess we all realise now she was living her dream through me.'

'That's right,' butted in Ray. 'She lived her life through you, and I tried to make her lighten a bit, so you had a life of your own, not just the horses. But you both seemed so determined, I gave up after a while.'

'Was that why we went on all those camping holidays that Mum hated?'

'You got it!'

'That makes sense in hindsight, Dad, I never realised. Did you feel side-lined?'

'Not so much as I was busy with the show. Then when the tragedy struck, it was all too late.'

Ethan and Sue turned their attention to Ray.

'That bit on the horse looks really clean Ray, what about the rest of it?'

Joanna looked and saw her dad had cleaned the hindquarters of the horse and was going around and around on the same area.

'What's going on here?'

'That's typical of me, going around and around in circles and never getting anywhere!'

'Can you explain that some more?'

'Well, for years I've been wanting to do new things and move on, but I haven't felt able to. First, it was pacifying Mia and then looking after Joanna.'

'But why not?'

'Because I have Joanna to look after and the show to run. I guess I feel trapped. Like when I got this horse collected and that little swine nipped me, life's like that, you think it's going along just right then something catches you up short.'

'But Dad, I'm 25, I haven't needed looking after for years, have I?'

'Of course not, but when you were younger I mean and then when you decided not to go to University and work on the show, I felt doubly tied again.'

'But you could have told me and gone anytime.'

'That was why I left you in charge this year, to see if I could.'

Joanna could see he was still grooming the same bit of the horse.

'But I thought I did okay. There were no major disasters and I sorted all the things that did arise.'

'You did well, Joanna; did I never say?'

'No'

'Oh, heavens, I'm so sorry.' He dropped the brush and hugged Joanna. There was a bit of a harrumph from the direction of Diane and they all turned to look. The somewhat subdued shetland stood surrounded in a sea of fallen winter coat. Where the other horses must have been clipped in the winter, he was still carrying his winter jumper. Diane was scratching away with a metal scraper.

'Diane is there something wrong?'

'I can't believe you left this horse with some much hair on him and haven't taken the old coat off. He's got lice under here and he needs a bath.'

'He's not ours, we borrowed him for this weekend because he's known for his personality. Would you like to bath him?'

'No, I've enough with horses at home.'

'So what else is bothering you? It's not just the state of his coat is it? You've been working up a real sweat?'

'I guess, if I have to be honest, I'm angry with myself. I've done these tasks before and I'm still making the same mistakes.'

'Mistakes?'

'Yeah, not sticking to the goal, and giving up too easily, taking the next best thing that comes along, as in catching this ratbag not the bay.'

'And does that relate to your life?'

'Oh, I know, it'll all come out anyway, Ray knows. I used to sleep around a lot and would take anything, wasn't fussy. But I thought I was over that now I'm getting married.'

There was a sharp intake of breath from Ray.

'So, I'm second best?'

'No, of course not, I mean that now I have made the choice for the best in life I'm frustrated that I can still make the old mistakes.'

'I'm not quite sure how to take that Diane.'

The two looked at each other. At that moment, a bell rang from the direction of the house.

'Saved by the bell! It's lunchtime, and I think this is a good moment to stop and take a break from this. It's proved an emotional morning for you all, and I want to continue to work with you all on these issues after lunch. Please, don't have arguments or discuss all this. Bear with us, as through the horses these are issues we can look at in a non-confrontational way, which will help you more in the long term. Will this work for you?' asked Ethan. They all acquiesced in their own way and made their way into the kitchen

# FIFTEEN

Lunch had been surprisingly pleasant as they all found they could talk a bit with each other as they were keeping off anything heavy. The afternoon session found them back in the indoor school. This time there were poles, jumps stands, all sorts of odd bits of equipment.

The four horses were wandering about and picking at some hay that had been put out for them. The shetland was looking damp and very moth-eaten.

Sue started, 'from this morning's sessions, I think we have made some ground in that you all seem friendlier! We will work through some of your issues in this afternoon's exercise which is all about the little problems that we meet in life. What we want you to do is build a course of three obstacles using what's in the arena. Now you can decide if you wish them to be a metaphor for something beforehand or we'll discuss it afterwards. We then want you to get a horse to go over the obstacles. You are not allowed to speak to each other, or the horses, you cannot touch each other or the horse, and no pretending to feed them as in pretending to have food in your pockets. Because this is something new, we will give you 15 minutes to discuss this; then ten minutes to set up. You carry out the task until you are satisfied that you have achieved it. Any questions?'

'That seems clear, can we ask you questions if they arise during the planning?' squeaked Joanna.

'Yes, but I can't guarantee the answer!' laughed Sue.

The three went into the arena to look at the equipment. Of course, the nosey shetland came over to help, and this time they found him amusing and he received strokes and rubs. They even all burst into laughter when he took off with a traffic cone in his mouth.

'So, how do we do this? 'said Ray.

'Well, I've not done this exercise before. It's a new one to me. I've no good plans at the moment,' answered Diane

'You must have some ideas?'

'We could make the jumps very small. They didn't say how big they must be,' she nevertheless continued.

'Or maybe put them very close together so they are practically one?' volunteered Ray.

'I can see a way,' said Joanna

'That's a good idea about making them one. What shall we use?' said Ray and he went to the heap and started rooting about.

'I've got an idea,' said Joanna

'I think we could use these wings to hold the poles up, just like proper jumps. They may be used to this,' added Diane.

'But there's an easier way, 'said Joanna more loudly, but the other two kept on rummaging and making ideas to each other. Finally, Joanna lost her temper.

'Will you two stop talking to each other and listen to me? Am I invisible or something? Am I not part of this group. Hey!'

They turned around in surprise and looked shamefaced.

'Sorry Joanna, I just guess we got carried away,'

'Like you've been ever since Christmas, you're so into each other that I don't seem to exist or matter any more! I've had enough of this. Nothing will change in this stupid therapy. I might just as well go home!' Joanna made to leave.

'Just typical of you Joanna, instead of staying and sorting things out, you run away again. Well just go and grow up!' shouted Diane with real anger.

'What do you mean run away?' yelled Joanna

'Like the time when we brought Challenger home and he wasn't happy; you just took off then ran away on holiday.'

'He wasn't happy, that horse was going to savage me. Don't think because I've been away from horses I've forgotten all about them. I was fully entitled to leave, you were all gawping at me as if I were some sort of villain. I didn't even want the stupid horse! And then after, not even one of you popped your head around the door to see if I was okay.'

'Why should we run after you, you spoilt child,' snapped Diane.

'Me a spoilt child? At least I didn't have to sleep around the neighbourhood because I'd lost a parent!' retorted Joanna with venom.

'You bitch! Go on run away, maybe it's going to snow!'

'Diane I wouldn't have minded about the snow. It was because you flipping well knew it would snow and you went anyway. All it needed was a quick chat about what to do in the eventuality. You made me give up my plans and never a thank you for the whole thing.'

'Is that true Diane?' asked Ray, looking thunderous.

'Well, I might have known about the snow...'

'What was the point of leaving Joanna in the dark; were you trying to show her up or something? You were the one who said we had to let her stew on her own after Challenger arrived. What's this all about Diane?'

'Because she's a spoilt bitch and she's not going to have you!'

'I'm not a spoilt bitch. I haven't done anything wrong. Since the announcement of your engagement, you two have ignored me, cut me out. You haven't even talked to me about what I feel about the whole thing.'

'See that proves my case, she's just trying to wreck everything.'

'That I am not! If either of you had bothered to talk to me, I could have told you how happy I was about the whole thing. Dad, you've been on your own for years. I would never stop you marrying again, but you've never talked to me. Now I am going because you two need to talk to each other. I'm out of here.'

'Joanna stop!' said Ray. 'I think I know why you act like this.' He sat down on a bale. 'As you know, your mum was very horse orientated before you were born, but her family never had the money for her to pursue a career with them. When you showed an interest she went over the top. She had you in leading rein classes practically before you could walk. That lead to some conflict as you wanted to play with friends and it led to you having quite a solitary life. Sometimes I would defy Mia when she got cross with you, and I'd take you out to the park or for an ice cream. In the end, you put two and two together and when she began to get cross about something, you would take yourself off and find me. I guess it became ingrained.

The camping trips didn't help, but at least we had some time together. Even when you went to school, we'd sometimes sneak off to the cinema. By the time we returned she would have calmed down, but she never did anything with you except horses. That's why, despite our pain when she died, we slipped into the cosy rut that we've had ever since then. When you gave up the horses it was even easier.'

Joanna found she was hugging the grey horse as he spoke, and memories came flooding back as he prompted them.

'So you're not spoilt, it was a damage tactic that hung on.' Yet as he spoke he was looking at Diane.

'That was quite a revelation all of you. This is a good moment to get back to the task, now that you've all let off a bit of steam. Let's see if you can work together', said Sue. Diane was very quiet and said nothing but the other two nodded. Finally, as Sue left, she asked Joanna, 'So what was your idea?'

'If we build a jumping lane down the side of the school with the three small jumps, we can then use this rope to coax or even scare the horses down. They didn't say the obstacles have to be free standing and they said a horse, not just one so it wouldn't matter if all went. They don't have to clear the jumps, so long as they go over…

'That sounds good, 'said Ray. 'Diane can you go with that?'

'Yes, I think I can,' she said unsmilingly. In the course building, she was quiet, and the chat was between Ray and Joanna, who found it so nice to be chatting with her dad again. Soon the course was built. They took the rope and made a line behind the horses who slowly moved off. Gently, they pushed them around the school until they were in front of the jumps. Smelling a rat, the grey jumped over the rope which had them all starting back in surprise, and the bay followed. They were looking at each other in consternation when they heard a guffaw from the side. They turned and looked. The shetland had taken himself down the lane, knocking the whole lot down but nevertheless, going over the obstacles.

'We're finished!' called Ray and they went over. There were some more chairs out and coffee and cake on a tray. They sank gratefully down and grabbed mugs.

'What was going on there?' asked Ethan.

'Well I guess that was a major clearing of the air,' said Ray. 'Diane and I have a few things to discuss I guess…'

'What was going on with the horses?'

'We tricked them at first, then the two big ones saw an easy way out as we left a gap, and the shetland in the meantime saved us.' said Joanna.

'Define saved us.'

'We had a problem which we hadn't seen, and he stepped in.'

'Does this relate to anything in your lives?'

'Well, for me, it reminded me of my dad, so often he would bring me a surprise gift when he came back off duty. Or when I was home he'd do the washing up which might have been my chore, for me,' Diane was struggling. 'He was always there for me, and I still miss him so much!' She burst into tears. Ethan gesticulated to Ray to let Diane alone as she sobbed into a hanky.

'I don't think my mum ever let me off anything,' said Joanna feeling envious. 'But sometimes she was good for a hug if something hadn't gone well in the ring. She went before I really hit teenage and Dad was there for me instead.'

'Yeah, well at least you've still got a dad.'

'And at least you've still got a mum!'

At which Diane looked up. 'You know I've never looked at it like that.'

The two looked each other in the eye for the first time in months.

'Well for me,' added Ray. 'It was like someone coming into my life and just taking some of the weight and responsibility off my shoulders. I wasn't the one that had to sort it for once.'

'But Dad, you only ever had to ask or say,' stated Joanna. 'I could do so much more.' Ray looked at Joanna as if seeing her afresh.

'I think this has been a very strong session for all of you, and tonight, we'll put it all together. Please all take some time out now and we'll meet for supper,' butted in Ethan.

# SIXTEEN

Joanna took the time to have a swim and a lie down on the bed. She missed the dogs; their hyperactive welcome, their movement and the way they were pleased to see her whatever mood she was in. Their gentle movements on the bed as they slept, and awakening with squeaky yawns. Supper was another feast, and afterwards, they all went into the sitting room where a bottle of wine was opened.

'How was today for you Diane?'

'Alright, I suppose. I have a lot to think about re my dad, I do think the horses were bolshy.'

'And what about the comment about taking second best in life? That hurt, 'said Ray.

'You misunderstand me. I was talking about my life before you; now I have the real thing, I can see the difference even more strongly.'

Joanna still had the feeling that Diane wasn't giving it all out; she was resisting something, but she didn't know what.

'Joanna, you had quite a breakthrough about some things in your life.'

'Well, I certainly hadn't been aware I was a spoilt brat; that I ran away from everything and my dad had resented all these years we've been running the show and making a career of it. Why have you never said anything, Dad? I'm shellshocked,' she said ruefully.

'Maybe I wasn't consciously aware of it and it's taken all this to put things into perspective for me. Yes, I have wanted to get away, and meeting Danny was the greatest thing that happened to me. But I also see that

Danny, you have manipulated me about Joanna and I don't understand why. I've been so besotted, that I hadn't seen what you were doing…and what I've been doing. I need some time to think this through.'

'You know, you can't have it all, Dad,' said Joanna bitterly,' You find me clingy, and you're suffocated, and you need to do things on your own. I would never have stopped you by being a brat; all you had to do was say so. When I got the dogs, you turned into some sort of tyrant because I did something that didn't involve your participation or permission. This needs to work both ways.'

'I'm sorry about that. I wanted to have a chat with you. I'd been worried about how you were feeling and there never seemed to be an opportunity.'

'I was only through the baize door.'

'I know that, but being in love makes you do all sorts of stupid things that you wouldn't normally.' Diane grabbed his hand at this, but he continued looking at Joanna.

'I think this will lead us all nicely into our last session in the morning. This is a very intense weekend. Breakfast will be a little later as we have the service in the chapel. After the last session, we'll have lunch, talk about what your next moves are, and then a fond farewell!'

With that Joanna, for herself felt dismissed and took herself to bed. She still didn't feel right with either of the others, but it was better than for months. Tomorrow she would have her dogs back. Yet it didn't stop her going around and around in her head all the conversations, actions and feelings. She slept badly, and at first light, was up and wandering around the garden.

She had reached a few conclusions. She and her dad had slipped into a rut, which neither of them had perceived and they needed to get out of it. Whether he had fallen for Diane as an unconscious thing, who would ever know? It was real to him, and she was happy for him. She would do all she could to help him be free as thanks for a recovered childhood. Her mum was a different figure now, even more bossy, less loving, more self-centered; who had lived her dreams through her daughter. What would the cost have been if she had lived? What had been buried and half acknowledged for years became clear.

Would Joanna have been a great show jumping success but under her mother's thumb? Or another embittered woman who hadn't quite made it? She'd never know. She was still sad about the loss of Mia, but also as she admitted to herself, relieved. Now, a great door was opening for herself, to do something new, something exciting. She must get out of her rut as well. She had a superb idea forming. And Diane? Joanna still couldn't get her head around Diane's antagonism to her when before she'd fallen for her dad, they'd been well on the way to re-kindling a friendship. Was it too much to build on those old grounds? What was the reasoning; was Diane even aware of what she was doing? The therapy had brought all these things into the open but seemed to have resolved little.

The beauty of the garden was comforting, but she wished she was taking a brisk walk with the Barknadoes. She always thought better as she strode along, it just wasn't the same. She made her way back indoors. As she climbed the stairs, she heard the sound of the sea. Waves breaking on the shore. She shook her head puzzled and made her way to the source of the noise. It was the chapel, but she had to look. She opened the door and found a small room, filled with this sound of the sea and on the back wall a projection of a beach with two sets of footsteps leading along it. Joanna was amazed, not what she would expect in a chapel at all. She went in and sat, absorbing herself in the sea scene. It seemed to be on a loop and after a while, she saw that the camera eye was following the footsteps in the sand. At some stage, she didn't see what happened, but the footsteps became one. Puzzled she sat and watched and watched.

She was then disturbed by people coming into the room. Oh no, the service, she wouldn't be able to escape.

'Hi Joanna,' a hand was placed on her shoulder and it was Sue. 'You don't have to stay,' she said as if reading Joanna's thoughts.

'No, I'd like to, I've been enjoying the sea,' said Joanna regretting her impulse as she said it. Sue smiled and sat next to her.

'It's just a simple half an hour service, just sit and enjoy!'

Then Ethan came to the front and sat on a chair by a table with a cross on it that Joanna had not even noticed before.

'Hi everyone, how's your week been?'

Some of the people in the room told tales of how they had been helping someone and there was a request for help with a garden in the village.

'Right now, let's sing together and praise his name.'

The screen came back on with the words to the songs and from around her, came the music. Thank heavens no guitar thought Joanna, but even so, she found herself singing along to the simple catchy tunes. The words seemed loving, kind and respectful, a far cry from the dirges in the local church.

Ethan began a talk, and it was about unconditional love, something that Joanna couldn't relate to. Why did God make people ill if he loved them and sent things to hurt them? Ethan likened him to a perfect parent, who would say when you boobed and was there with a hug when needed and never turned his back. Joanna humpfed to herself.

'Now finally, I found this video on the internet, and of course, God is not like a dog. He gave us creatures as our companions, and maybe they echo a little of what he has for us.'

Up came a simple black and white cartoon with a song about the divine God and canine mutt. How God forgives and in an echo of this, the dog wags his tail and how it's us who turns away, not them. Joanna saw her dogs when they ecstatically greeted her when she came back from being out. She saw how we can't match their love for us. It was so simple, and the words broke Joanna who began to sob.

Not in over sentimental emotion, but because she could see her dogs, how she was with them and how they loved her, how there could be a greater, wonderful, parental love that the dogs echoed. She wanted a mother and a father. Sue's arm came around Joanna's shoulder and she didn't take in much more of the service. She was aware when the people left, and Sue gave her another tissue.

'That's what people miss about God, in an imperfect world, the perfect parent. How do you feel? I can ask you now that we're not doing therapy, 'asked Sue gently.

'Overwhelmed, drained, but also something in me feels freed up,' sniffed Joanna.' I need to know more, is this true? It doesn't tie in with any of my experiences with church.'

'Well, that's religion, not true Christianity. We've tied ourselves up in knots over the years and lost the true way.'

'This sounds familiar. I've had Chloe try to talk about me like this, but it never made sense.'

'Well, she's been part of our house church network since it started. We're under the banner of what's known as the Evangelical Alliance and the Anglican church, so we're not nutters!'

Joanna grinned, 'Oh boy, am I going to eat humble pie when I get home.' They laughed.

'Look, here's a Bible to read, just read the Gospels first, they tell it all, then chat with Chloe even if your face is red.'

'You know, I think I might well do that.' Joanna noticed that the beach was playing on the wall again.

'Why is there suddenly only one set of footprints?'

'It's not strictly a Bible quote, but it's a picture of our life with God and how we walk together, and sometimes, he picks us up and carries us...'

Later, Joanna felt content after a good breakfast; the others were cheerful too. She looked forward to the next session, even if just to see what might happen. The same three horses were in the school and there was one small jump already laid out.

'Right now,' said Ethan. 'Your task today is all about teamwork,' The three looked and grimaced at each other. 'There is always a leader in a team and sometimes they are a good leader and sometimes not. This will be a talking exercise! Your task is to collect and halter one of the horses, and then take it over the small jump. Sounds easy? Well, you're all going to be a very close team, taking down some of the limits of body space. You're going to link arms with Joanna in the middle. So effectively, you have two hands controlled by the Boss. There's always a right and left-hand man. Joanna, give directions to your limbs so they can do the tasks, such as 'right hand pick up the halter,' but the workers cannot reply. Do you get it?' They looked dubiously at each other then nodded; it seemed most odd.

'Right off you go, no preparation, just go for it!'

Linked arms, they stood for a moment and Joanna realised she had to command.

'Right arm, please pick up the halter, and we'll walk towards the chestnut horse.'

This was easily done. Then it got messy as Joanna had to tell each hand what to do.

'Right hand put the nose through the head collar, left-hand help to pull the halter over the head and bring the lash over so we can do the buckle up.' Telling two hands how to buckle up got her in giggles as they tried to put the two pieces together. Then she noticed that the left hand wasn't taking her orders to put the leather through the buckle.

'Left hand, please do as I say. Hold the buckle upright so the other hand can push the leather through.' Joanna became steadily more assertive.

She could feel left hand's body getting stiffer and stiffer as she gave the commands. After the patient horse had the headcollar on, Joanna realised there was no rope.

'Team, Boss admits she forgot the rope, we need to go and get the long one from the corner. Left hand, please hold the noseband and bring the horse with us.'

Left hand obeyed but began to march ahead of the rest of the body, beginning to pull them along.

'Left hand, please slow down, the rest of the body can't keep up.' Left hand suddenly let go of the horse and swung around.

'I'm not doing this stupid exercise and I'm not taking orders from you!'

Ray and Joanna stood open-mouthed.

'Why should you tell me what to do, who do you think you are? I'll take orders from Ray, but not you!'

With that, she released the horse, who, reacting to the outburst of emotion, swung around and nearly knocked Ray flying as it took off. For a split second, they all just stood there.

'Just take your hands off him. Joanna, stop trying to be my friend. You can't have him, he's mine.' A look of horror came across her face as she realised what she had said. Joanna backed away. So that was what it was all about. Diane really wanted Ray all to herself. What had been passed over yesterday now was finally out in the open.

'I think it would be a good moment to come out of the arena and let the horses calm down,' intervened Sue. They all suddenly saw that the horses following the lead of the grey, were galloping around the school and in their direction. They stood in silence watching what had started as a fear reaction, turn into an excuse to let off steam as the horses cavorted, bucked and farted. Eventually they calmed down and went to stand in a corner snorting and huffing about their workout.

'What went on there with the horses?'

'I think they reacted to Diane's anger and outburst,' said Ray. 'But just look at them now, they've calmed down and are back to normal.'

'Do you think this reflects what has just happened?'

'What now that Diane has come clean we'll get back to normal…I don't think so,' said Joanna.

'Why not?'

'Because Ray's my dad, he'll never stop being so. I don't see how she could think he would stop. I will always be there, she has to get over it.' Joanna glared at Diane.

'Joanna, I'm sorry, I had no idea that I had this agenda. It came spilling out, something here triggered it. I know full well that I have to share Ray.'

'Share? Why share? He's not a packet of biscuits. Why look at it that way? It's a new start for all of us. If you had talked instead of bottling it up, none of this would have happened.'

'Um, I resent being talked about like a digestive, but Joanna is right, we need to talk all this through. We seem to have formed a dysfunctional family before there was even a marriage.'

'He's also not a replacement for your dad. I've never seen Chloe as one for Mia, is that why you want him to yourself, are you scared to lose him?'

There was a silence as what Joanna said hit home.

'He's not going to disappear, he's here to stay.'

'Oh, I know, I know, the head gets it, but something inside is adrift Joanna.'

'I think this is a good time to make our way to the house and have a chat together over lunch. I think we have some ideas to help you.' said Sue

It seemed like they were all back at square one as they ate a roast lunch in near silence. The conversation needed a kickstart.

'I think that you three have just had one of the most powerful and emotional weekends of your lives,' began Ethan. 'A lot has come to the surface that needs to be looked at. Joanna, I think maybe you have had the most positive experience in some ways. You have some new ideas about your mother and your relationship with Ray. The most negative has been between you and Diane. Ray, the deepest things that have come out are the issues on the lack of communication between you and Joanna, but I guess they're things that are easily resolved. Diane, I think we have things to sort out most with you and your relationships both with Joanna and Ray. I would like to invite you and Ray to stay on a few more days and have some counselling that will help you with these issues and your upcoming marriage. I think Joanna will find these things resolved without her immediate involvement.' He leant back and waited for reactions.

'If you think I'm staying for more beating me up and blaming me for everything, then you've another thing coming!' snapped Diane and she began to rise from her seat.

'Now stop,' said Ray, putting a forceful hand on Diane's arm. 'There's no way I'm going home and going ahead with our marriage with us all still at loggerheads over things, and you so unhappy. Stay?'

'Are you saying it's all off if I don't?' shouted Diane.

'Yes.'

## Challenger

She sat down, and they let her think.
'I don't have any choice do I?'

# SEVENTEEN

Joanna could hear Chloe getting the dogs to be quiet while she waited outside the front door. It opened, and she was engulfed in a Chloe hug then they were knocked to the floor as the Barknadoes hit in full power. There was nothing either could do under the mass attack of licking, barking, jumping about and general wiggling. They endured then slowly sat up.

'Now that's what I call a homecoming!' laughed Joanna and struggled to her feet. The dogs, if they could, would have wrapped themselves around her.

'Thanks so much for looking after them!'

'I enjoyed every minute and they were beautifully behaved,' and she cast an eye at them. 'Well, most of the time! Coffee or a hot chocolate?'

'Oh, chocolate please!'

They went into the kitchen dodging dogs and Joanna slumped at the table. It had been a long day.

'Tell me all or do you want to wait until the morning?'

'Morning?'

'Yes, you're not going back to that cold old house on your own, the spare bed's made up.'

It seemed a brilliant idea.

'Thanks, I'll stay. After all, let me tell you all now, while it's all fresh in my mind.'

Over several hot chocolates and until late in the evening, Joanna told Chloe everything, trying not to spare herself, to be honest, and paint a true picture. Finally, she finished.

'Phew, you've had a powerful time, and are you happier?'

'Yes, I sense something has changed. Although I've not processed things, I am different if not happy. I need to chat with Dad and we need to sort some things, and Diane too. But with her, I feel there are still some things we need to sort. And the church thing was amazing, I'm sorry I dismissed you all this time, it's caught my interest and I want more.'

'Ethan's group is one of many around the country.'

'Yes, he told me, it's certainly not what I expected, and I loved the bit with the footsteps along the sand.'

'That's a very famous picture and verse, it's related to lots of Jesus's sayings. Not all the groups are the same. Ethan's more into technology than some, but we all adhere to a set of core Biblical beliefs…I'm sorry, you're fading and I was getting on my hobby horse!'

With that Joanna took to bed with two wriggly, happy bed shovers who had no effect on her as she slipped into a deep, untroubled sleep. Early in the morning, the dogs woke her asking to go out and she met Chloe in the kitchen.

'I take it you slept well?'

'Like a log, but it's Monday, now I must get my act together and check on the office. Are the horses okay?'

'There's been a band of about ten girls who've been sleeping over and I think the horses and stables will be shining they've done so much. They got some riding in too, there's a woman with an AI qualification, so yes, all is fine! It's half term, so they're pleased to have the extra time. Diane rang and sort that out.'

'That's good to know!'

'There is one slight problem, on the day you need me to dog sit again, I have to go to Wales and sign papers to complete on the new cottage. I decided that I must distance myself a bit from Diane straight after she's wed so she can find her own feet and not be hampered by me!'

'Oh, I'm sure that's not the case. I knew you weren't settled here, but I think it's right for you to be back among all the people you know so well, and I'll miss you now we seem to have got over all the blips.'

Joanna was engulfed in yet another Chloe hug.

'I'll be around until the wedding, and then they'll be off on the honeymoon. I'll introduce you to another house church nearby, and you can make your own way from there, oh, Guy, your dog trainer goes to it too.'

Joanna's eyes widened, 'I'd never have thought he was like that, but I guess it makes sense! I wonder if he could have the dogs for me?'

They breakfasted together and after fond farewells, Joanna packed the dogs into the car and popped around to the office. Sheila was in and Joanna found everything fine, it seemed that she had been away forever. It felt like she must take some form of control. Sheila seemed to be coming into her own having been left in charge a lot more recently. She wasn't as stressed as earlier and she had gained an air of authority about her. Thoughtfully, Joanna left and drove to Guy's place, realising she was putting off going home for as long as possible by not phoning him.

She had long known the Estate manager's cottage but was surprised to find how much work had been done on it. There were new roof tiles and the walls had been painted in a deep cream. Thankfully, Guy's car was parked outside, and shushing the dogs she went to ring the bell. Guy answered with a surprised look on his face,

'What brings you to my neck of the woods? Are the dogs all right? Chloe said you'd been away.' At the sound of his voice, they, of course, began to bark.

'Let them out, they can tear around the paddock and garden.'

The two leapt about with delight in the new smells and room to charge about.

'I guess you need something to be here? Have you seen this place since it was done up, come and see?'

Joanna followed him in and found the cottage done out in its original Victorian style with the range burning in the main room. She could see through the door that the scullery was new and modern although disguised as Victorian.

'This is amazing. It's so real but modern. Did you do all this work? I don't remember Dad talking about doing this.'

'Well the Victorian era is my thing, and when Chloe found this place for me, it was under the agreement that I did it up to let as a holiday home.'

Joanna was startled; she really had been kept out of the loop of things even before Diane had arrived. So, he was doing things behind her back, despite all he said!

'Oh, so you must think my place needs a bit of TLC!'

'Oh, I love your house. It's all still there, never been touched.'

'So, it wasn't too irksome coming to teach the dogs then.'

Guy had the grace to look a bit red,' Well I had some sneaky looks.'

'Next time, we'll do a guided tour, there are parts I haven't looked at for years!'

'So why do I have the pleasure of this visit?' Guy was suddenly politely formal.

'I need to do one more session at the Record office and I don't have a dog sitter. Is there any chance you could have them from 8 to 3 on Wednesday? It's too long to leave them alone.'

'You mean they might have eaten the house?'

'Something like that!'

'Shouldn't be a problem…maybe I should branch out into dog boarding, the original kennels are still at the back. Come and have a look.'

Joanna followed him through the scullery and out the back found the old pigsty, outbuildings and kennels, still with their runs intact.

'They knew how to build things to last in those days.'

They looked inside to find large inner rooms with benches.

'Would need a bit of work with some light and heat and maybe a roof, but there's a possibility isn't there?! It's a shame that I only have a short lease.' Guy turned to Joanna, seeming more animated than he had ever done.

'You're more of a businessman than I thought!' she laughed. 'But don't lock my two up in there yet! What would you do when you need to do classes and things? You can't leave the premises if there are valuable dogs here; so many are being stolen these days, it's all over Facebook.' Guy looked taken back at her frankness.

Right on cue the dogs came running around the corner, both covered in mud and wet.

'Looks like they found the mill pond!'

'Is it still full?'

'Come and see.'

Joanna followed Guy down the path to the old mill. She hadn't been there since she was a teenager. It had been one of the places she and her friends had hung out in those long school holiday summers. It brought back memories of those times filled with laughter, finding love and friendship; a bond that still held now with those who had stayed behind. The building itself needed a new roof and the windows were falling out. The trees had grown, deepening the shade. But the pond was as deep and mysterious as it had ever been. There was a sensuous feeling to the place.

'I had a lot of fun here when I was a teenager!' blurted Joanna.

Guy raised an eyebrow at her.

'Not like that!' Now it was Joanna's turn to go red. 'We would meet here on hot summer days, we'd swim and talk about life and boys…' She was going redder.

'Maybe you need to put that shovel down, Joanna!' Guy smiled, and she suddenly took in how his green eyes were sensuous like the pool itself. She pulled herself together, still feeling swamped by her memories and a new, undefined emotion.

'Well, maybe we need to do something with this building too. There's so much on this estate that was built by my great grandparents after the fire.' Joanna became businesslike too.

'Not a Victorian theme park?'

'Urgh no, but something sensitive, yet at the same time cashing in as the National Trust does!'

They jumped as the dogs leapt into the pond again, thrashing around and getting covered in weed.

'Trust them to ruin the atmosphere!' laughed Joanna.

The dogs got out and ran around the place like a pair of lunatics. Joanna and Guy followed them back through the wood to the house, chatting about dogs and the other people at the dog school. Guy still gave little away about himself but was friendlier that he had ever been. Joanna wondered if the jobs-worth security guard still lingered somewhere about. Then she had a brilliant idea.

'Why don't you come up later this afternoon and look around? The house is empty and I'm not sure when Dad's back, so it may be the best time.'

'Why not?' Guy really smiled.' About 5?'

# EIGHTEEN

Joanna made her way home with two soggy dogs. She wondered how long Diane would be away as she guessed the Penelopes' half-term must soon be over. She popped down to the stables were she found Ann, the AI taking a jumping lesson in the arena. Joanna leant on the rails in the now familiar manner and watched for a minute, Jack and Jill were actually sitting quietly too. Ann saw her and came over.

'Hi, I'm Joanna, just checking to see if all's OK and if you had heard from Diane about when she'll be back.' As she was saying it, Joanna realised how bad that sounded. Surely, she should be the one to know? Just what was she doing, all this wasn't any of her business? Maybe she was trying again to have some form of control? Yet the thought flittered away.

'I had a phone call last night, they're back on Sunday night, time's in well with the end of half term.'

'Have you all had fun?'

'You know I have, I might even talk to Diane about doing some freelance teaching here, it's a bit like getting back on a bike, you don't forget!'

'Your niece will be happy then!'

'Please don't tell her, she's been on at me for the past couple of years for a pony!'

They laughed, and Joanna made her escape. Sunday would be the end of her freedom. Her stomach clutched a bit; she had to talk to Ray and the thought of making peace with Diane had her walking very briskly up the lane. One of the horses was near the fence and she realised it was Challenger.

Fresh with her therapy feeling and the new excitement, she wondered if he would now forgive her, so she called him over. He pricked up his ears and came over with that familiar long stride. This time he came and sniffed her through the fence; no nastiness and Joanna began to hope that he had forgiven her for whatever he had seen in her, or it was gone. But no, he gave a snort as if disgusted and turned his back and walked away. So, she wasn't there yet with him, but she trusted his judgement; he had seen her unhappiness and had reacted in a surprising way. He had seen through her and it had all been born out by the therapy work.

Maybe when she had made her peace, he'd forgive her. She suddenly wanted her old horse back and that had the worry rising. No riding, she would be straight back to wanting to do better and better then she'd end up back at square one; a pot hunting maniac. She couldn't go back there. She took off up the track, walking until she was breathless, and it took her mind off things. The dogs thought it great and ran up and down like maniacs hunting in the hedges and jumping in and out of the ditches, completely forgetting their already active day. They were all wet and panting by the time they marched back in the house.

Joanna let the dogs in and the smell of home; a musty, doggy, old smell, utterly familiar and yet new as she had never noticed it before. And the feelings that came with it. Tears started in her eyes as the emotions and everything she had thought about and experienced welled up. But the dogs didn't let her stay and wallow for too long, insisting that they needed a second breakfast. They barked and jumped until they got their way. Joanna looked at her house again with new eyes and saw how dark and neglected it seemed. She went through the baize door and saw everything with new eyes. The house hadn't been decorated since her mother's time. Her home needed some TLC and money spent on it. It would be almost embarrassing to show Guy around. These days there seemed to always be some enormous rug being pulled from under her feet. She needed so much to talk this all through with Ray. Would he return and still have no time for her? Had she really held him back all this time? What a mess they'd made of things. Did he understand that she didn't mind his marrying Diane? How would it all work with her? It would take some courage to talk and make a new start with her deadly stepmother! That thought at least made her grin.

Later, Joanna was surprised by her own reactions as she waited for Guy. She'd even put clean jeans with a smart top on and had tied her hair back. She almost had butterflies. She didn't want to go there; into what she was feeling or doing. There was too much going on, she didn't want any complications until Challenger approved her. She began to realise how much that meant to her. Yet it didn't stop her having a quick glimpse in the hall mirror when she went to answer the door. Guy also appeared apprehensive, but cheerful.

'I've been looking forward to this! I take it we can take our time and I can bore you with my observations?'

Joanna nodded, and they entered the porch. And he was off.

'Wow just see the tiles in here!' he exclaimed.

'I used to pretend this was a lift when I was a kid.' Joanna smiled at the sudden recollection. 'In that umbrella stand are three spiders in there. They've been there for years, they're almost tarantulas!'

'Ugh, no thanks!'

They went into the hall and Guy looked around him.

'This really needs that skylight on the little landing doesn't it, clever use of light. They certainly knew their stuff.'

Joanna led him into the sitting room on the left. He inspected the parquet floor tiles and the ceramic tiles around the fireplace, and the odd room divider.

'I'm not sure if this is the original wall, but they would have had sliding doors here which they could pull back for dancing, but there doesn't seem a lot of space here. It's smaller than usual, most interesting in such a large house. Three big reception rooms, Morning room, study, parlour and a dining room. Fascinating.'

'The room behind used to be my playroom, maybe someone has changed it in the past to have a morning room there.'

'Wow, all these sash windows, and the three bay windows, Joanna, I'm in heaven!'

'Well, we haven't started yet!'

They went down the hall, to her playroom. It had French windows out into the garden at which point the dogs realised Guy was there and jumped at the door to come in. They hurtled in but they didn't give him a dusting over; they loved him.

'I used to sit with Mia on these steps and pods peas sometimes, and she would try to scare me with ghost stories. We had an old record player in here and a horsehair sofa with a hole in it. It was only when I realised that a lot of hair would have come from the slaughterhouse that I wouldn't sit on it any more.' It surprised Joanna at how these recollections were bursting through.

'Now at the back is the big sitting room, or as I used to think, the ballroom. It's empty now, as you know, we just use it at Christmas.'

Memories of Christmas parties past flashed through her mind. The room had more light than the other rooms, Joanna wondered why it wasn't used then saw there were no radiators. Guy grabbed her hand,

'Would Madame care to dance?'

Before she could reply, his hands came around her waist and he spun her round into a giddying waltz.

Joanna was relieved that she had done a ballroom dancing course at school and could allow herself to be swept around and not fall flat on her face or tread on his toes. She remembered the touch of him from the Christmas party. Soon dizzy, they stopped.

'Sir, we haven't been formally introduced,' Joanna gasped, giddy in body and soul. 'Unhand me, sir!' Though she didn't mean it in the slightest.

'My wish is your command,' and he let go so quickly Joanna nearly did fall over and he caught her again,

'I think my lady complains too loudly!'

They both laughed, and the dogs jumped up at them wanting to be part of the action. Joanna was both breathless and wound up in an odd sort of way.

'Where does that door lead?' Guy asked, back on his mission.

'Into the kitchen area and servants' wing, and my side.'

'So maybe this was a dining room?'

'Could be, but we use the other room.'

Joanna lead Guy back down the hallway

'Hey, a baize door! Wow, never seen mouldings like this, and it still swings!'

'Don't break it, it's had a lot of use over the years!'

To the left of the hall past the stairs they went into their dining room. Like a kid, Guy was at the windows, fiddling with the old wooden blinds that still worked and checking the old gas light fittings that had been left as decoration.

'I don't like that heater!' he exclaimed.

'It was installed in the 50s, and it heats the water, don't moan at it!'

Joanna was glad that all the time Guy was enjoying himself, not noticing the peeling paper in places, shabby furniture, the wobbly floorboards or the general untidiness. He was into the kitchen behind, opening all the creamy painted cupboards and muttering to himself.

'What's up now?'

'I'm not sure that this has always been a kitchen, although these cupboards are of the era. Look behind the sink and the window, there's a huge gap where the units are so tall. Or maybe this is all just newer fittings. I'll have to think about that one….'

'Right come on,' Joanna was getting agitated at all these ponderings; this was her home. 'Here we have the back door, the loo and the pantry, all this in original groovy dark green and cream and quarry tiles to go! Through that door is the cellar and archive, maybe we can look at that later. The baize door is just on the other side of this door which is kept locked to make it my flat. We think all this was the servants' quarters but is now my end. As you know not much original décor remains.' Joanna unlocked the door.

'I know this bit, your kitchen sitting room, the gun room and the storerooms with the ballroom door on the left. I think maybe that was the original kitchen. I do love these little mysteries.'

'Right, upstairs in the posh side then?'

'Lead on!' As they went up the stairs, Guy was lovingly running his hand on the bannister. On the little landing, they stared up at the skylight.

'It leaks?'

'But of course.'

Up three more steps, they were at the bedrooms.

'This pink room has a little bay window that faces the garden. And I was born in here.' She opened the door and let him peek in. Joanna was surprised at how protective she felt about it, even though it was now Ray and Diane's room.

'The next one must have been the master because this door in it leads into the dressing room that used to be mine. No comments on my taste in décor or posters, please. They both went in and looked out of the window which showed the view down the valley.

'I used to listen to the screech owls in the nights when I was a kid.'

But Guy was investigating the wardrobe.

'Original and built in.'

Joanna shut its door. 'Um, personal stuff in there.'

'Sorry, overstepping the mark.'

They left the difficult ground and went into the next room.

'I guess it's just the same as the dining room with the three windows.'

'Certainly seems so.' They shut the door and went to the last room.

'I often wonder who ended up in this one. All you can see is the brick wall of the next house, it never gets any light.'

'Maybe a governess or some doddery relative they had to home? I will have to find my floor plans and dig about. Maybe you should see what the Record office has...'

'We have most of the original documents in the archive,' said Joanna proudly.

'Then I must book some time to have a look!'

They went down the stairs to the little landing and back up three. On the right was a loo, then a bathroom with black and white lino.

'I don't know if this is an original bathroom, but it was done up again in the 50s when the original heating was put in.'

'And when was the corridor blocked up?'

'Again, we did it when I wanted that half to be my own self-contained flat. It leads through to another corridor, with a box room, bathroom, another sitting room and my bedroom. All on different levels. I never understood why do you know?'

'You've caught me out there, my research head is kicking in. It's not such a big place for an important family.'

'I think they were just glad when the old place burnt down, that was huge and there are a couple of paintings of it. It must have been a nightmare to keep up.'

'Could we just peep at these rooms, then maybe it's time for a drink, I could do with a pint!?'

'Sounds good to me!'

They went back down and round, but she only let Guy glance in for a second into her bedroom, her bathroom and the other room was full of boxes and old furniture. There was something going on inside her, this having to show a stranger her nest was unsettling, but he was so amiable, his enthusiasm was catching. If she did the house up he would be a great help, and she suddenly saw a picture of them restoring the Victorian splendour. As they walked out, dogs eagerly following they saw Challenger in the paddock.

'That horse really didn't like you did it?'

'I think he reads me, and when I'm not right, he just reflects my emotions. But our therapy weekend away helped. I can see so much more on how my life is going. I'll be glad when the wedding is over, and I can get my act together.' She wasn't going to give him any more details though!

'Dogs do that for us too, that's why there are so many pat dogs and hospital visiting dogs. I help out sometimes with an animal shelter. How people can do such things to them is beyond me.' Joanna saw him shudder and changed the subject.

'These two certainly know when I'm hungry, they're at the pantry door before I am!!' They laughed and entered the cosy pub. The dogs sat quietly for once under the table.

'Thank you, Joanna, I'm aware that parts of that were intensely private, I hope I didn't intrude.'

'No, it was quite surprising how protective I felt about the rooms. I've never seen them with a strangers' eye before. I was surprised at the memories that came back too. I suppose I've taken the place for granted. I will one day have a plaque on the wall saying I was born here, but I'm not quite sure what for.'

'Not so many people are born at home any more.'

'Why are you so fascinated by the Victorian era?'

'I grew up in the two up two down version of this in Aldershot; my parents ran a B&B. They ripped a lot of the old stuff out, so maybe it's a Freudian wanting to get it all back again! I did my dissertation on Victorian architecture for my degree. Not much use as I wasn't going to be an architect or anything.'

'Are they still running it?'

'No, they both passed on about ten years ago, we were never close.'

'I'm glad you didn't remark on what a state my place is in, I never noticed that until lately.'

'But it means a lot it's left intact, fantastic for the historian in me.'

The wine was loosening Joanna's tongue. 'I think maybe that we must decide what to do with it. Either walk away and let someone do it up or make it a major new project. We seem to have been sleepwalking since my mother died. So much is changing and going on in my head lately, I'm feeling overwhelmed.' Joanna nearly bit her tongue at that, she had never expected to open up to Guy like this.

'You wouldn't sell it? It's part of your history and inheritance! That would be dreadful.'

'I don't know. When I think of people who live in the same place all their lives, doing the same thing, I feel claustrophobic and want to run away. Dad and I will have to talk about it when he gets back. And I know that I understand precious little of my history. I catalogued and stored all those papers, plans and books, but didn't look at what they meant, what they were telling me. Now I want to go back and read them all in a new light. And I want to start the new business. But the wedding's soon and oh, crumbs, I've got all that to deal with.'

'Maybe we could look at the archive together, I'd love to see the design and the accounts and who built it and so on…and I think there is a bit of a mystery there too. Have you ever been in the attic?'

'I never knew there was one! There must be a hatch somewhere if so. Does this mean you're just taking me out for a drink to get your hands on my archive, shame on you!'

'You've found me out!' For once he really laughed. Two small faces peered quizzically up at him.

'Do you fancy something to eat?'

'Could do!'

They ordered and ate and drank some more wine, then made their way in the darkness back to the house. It was nice just to chat about this and that, she could take her mind off the wedding, the family and everything for a while and it was a huge relief.

'I'm glad I only have farm tracks to drive back on,' said Guy a little slurrily, 'let me see you to your door, Madame.'

'Oh Sir, not the main door for me, I'm at the back in the servant's wing.'

They giggled out of all proportion to the humour and Joanna let the dogs in.

'Thank you for a lovely evening Guy.'

'My pleasure! Will you be at the class next week?'

'Not until after the wedding, I've a feeling next week is going to be crazy. But could you ask if anyone on the course could dog sit for me on that day? Everyone is going in the village.'

'I'll try!'

He turned abruptly and went as if Joanna had said something to offend him. After all this evening when he had finally opened up, showing what he was really like. So, no goodnight kiss thought Joanna a bit giddily, well, there was always the wedding…

# NINETEEN

Wednesday dawned cold with storms and heavy rain. It suited Joanna's mood down to the ground. Too much time spent mooching about the house, as yet again she wasn't needed in the office for the moment, and there was only so much dog walking she could stand. Her idea for Harry was going around and around in her head. One minute it seemed like pure genius and then next a waste of time, doomed to failure. When she dropped the dogs off at Guy's, he seemed to have reverted to security man and took the dogs without a word or smile, not even remarking on the new harnesses she had bought.

She drove through heavy rain and traffic which suited her mood, what was the matter with Guy? On arrival at the Record office, she found Harry had left her a diary to summarise, which completely took her out of herself. It was by one of the wealthy, pioneering Eighteenth-century English women who had travelled the world. In Russia, she remarked about the outriders to the carriages, who ran in front to clear the way, who unsurprisingly, didn't live for long. Later, she met Nelson, and what she had to say about him and Emma Hamilton was a revelation. Joanna made notes to see how it would tie in with her records. Sadly, there was only one year's diary and the job only kept her going till lunchtime, so she went to see if Harry was in the office. When he appeared, he too seemed a bit stressed.

'Sorry not to meet you, another staff meeting with usual infighting, it is getting beyond a joke. Also, Jan will be joining us, is that a problem?'

Joanna had no idea who Jan was, so she shrugged no problem and they went to the cafe around the corner.

'Harry, I've got an idea that I think you might find interesting,' said Joanna as they sat down.

'Tell me, I'm all ears,' said Harry. 'After this morning's debacle, I'm ready to do something new.'

Joanna's spirits lifted.

'While I was in Wales, the place we were in had all their documents in a heap in the library and I saw some that were torn and stained.'

'The budding archivist in you told them off and put them in a box?' laughed Harry.

'Not at all, it just struck me….'

At that moment, a tall man in a business suit came to the table. Harry rose and kissed him on the cheek.

'Hi Jan, how was the journey down?'

'M25 a car park as usual.'

Joanna took this time to gather her wits together, oh no, she had never realised that Harry was gay, any little thoughts that she had of them together hurtled out the window, and she readjusted her mindset. She turned to Jan and proffered her hand,

'Hi, I'm Joanna, Harry's been teaching me the ropes at the office.'

Jan smiled, and not for the first time Joanna thought what a waste it was that there just seemed to be so many good looking gay men around!

'Nice to meet you, sorry to disrupt your tete a tete.'

'Not at all.'

Jan sat, and they read the menus, ordered and in the quiet pause, before the drinks arrived, Harry returned to what Joanna was telling him.

'I saw these documents, and it took me back to how many aren't accepted here and how family history is the big thing now, to say the least. What about offering a service, showing people how to catalogue and use their family records? It drives me mad to think that things are being lost because our present perceptions can't tell what will be important in ten or twenty years time. Or all those voice tapes and film we sent back that within a few years we could scrub all the background interference off. We could advertise. Think of how many Record offices there are all over the country; if we could win the establishment over, it could snowball!' Joanna saw Jan raise an eyebrow at Harry.

'With all the contacts in this office, we could find our first customers there. We could even store stuff ourselves for people when they go…'

Joanna looked at them, they were mulling it over.

'As you know, we do already make visits,' said Harry. 'But we don't advertise or make a service of it.'

'It would mean a lot of travelling if it took off.'

'I know, that's the bit I'm not so keen on with the dogs.'

The two men looked at each other again.

'I could take a qualification in document storage, and data management. I've found several already.'

'I think you may have a brilliant idea!' Jan said finally, grinning at Harry. 'You've been wanting out for a while, and as an Archivist, you'll have clout. I like the travelling, so that's not a problem. Sorry, Joanna, I didn't say, I work in data management, which is a bit similar I suppose. Maybe you could focus on the actual documents. I work in an office north of London and this might just mean we could work together, and it would make living much, much easier, Harry?'

'It could well be a solution, but we'll have to make a business plan, maybe start slowly. I could stay on at the office part time, so we have an income until it supports us. Joanna, you will be still working on the show, won't you? And as your collection will be online at last next month, you'll begin to get contacts that way. Hey, this could be good!' Harry grinned, and Joanna realised he hadn't seemed so happy since Christmas.

The meal was then spent dotting figures and plans and timescales on pieces of paper. Then agreeing to meet after the wedding and go through it all again after they'd all done some more research. Harry would go undercover at the office to see if there was a way to get the rejects sent to him. Back at the office Joanna met the boss again and they celebrated her records joining theirs with cake and tea, and before long she was winding her way back to the dogs and gloomy Guy. Yet her brain was on overdrive, with ideas and things she needed to check. She hadn't felt so excited for a long time.

'Good grief, what on earth have you been up to today?' was Guy's question as she came through the door, and she suddenly knew of bouncing a bit. The Barknadoes came tearing in having heard her voice. This time she was ready for them and met them at their level, trying to keep them from totally flooring her. At the back of her mind was that she was being watched by her teacher. They calmed quickly and sat at her feet looking their best adorable for a moment then wandered off.

'I've just had the most marvellous meeting with Harry and Jan. We've got a really good business idea and I think it may work. It's all to do with the documents and storage and helping people to store and record their own ones that the Record office won't take. They reject some now because of quality and that may all change in a few years, and I'll be able to work from home and it's just fantastic!' Joanna realised she was out of breath.

'You sound like that flipping advert!' Guy was smiling though, apparently in friendly mode.

'How was it with the beasts?'

'I enjoyed having them around the house, makes me realise how much I miss having a dog. I will really have to think seriously about getting one of my own again.'

'What do I owe you for your professional services? Joanna nearly bit back the comment, she didn't want security man to return.

'Nothing I've enjoyed it. I've also had a quick search for some plans of the layouts of houses and I want to show you how they worked. I've got the real names for the rooms for you and what they were used for.' He began to rummage around on the table. Jill rushed in and Joanna saw she still had her walk harness on and bent to take it off. But Jill wasn't having anything of it. She twirled and barked and tried to get away, completely not herself.

'Jill be quiet!' Joanna shouted, but to no avail, forgetting all the training. Then she realised Jack wasn't there.

'Where's Jack?' Jill took off to the back door.

'This looks like he's up to something again. I suppose this is a classic Lassie moment and we have to follow,' laughed Joanna and went to follow Jill. She ran barking past the kennels and down to the mill. The way was wet and slippery in the growing darkness.

Joanna could hear the millrace thundering. This wasn't good. They got to the Mill and the water was flooding over the pond which was filled with bits of trees and rubbish. Joanna had never seen the water so high. Jill was barking at a tree caught on the weir which was twisting and turning in the flow. Then Joanna saw it, the bright red of Jack's harness against the tree. Joanna screamed, 'Jack' but in the dim light couldn't see much. Guy climbed over the edge of the weir into the water

'Guy don't be stupid, it's just his harness.'

But Guy, bracing himself against the flow was wrestling with it, and suddenly it came free and Joanna saw it wasn't.

'Quick, come and take him, I can't manage it all on my own.'

Joanna leapt at the anger in Guy's voice and got in the bitterly cold water too, it was difficult to keep her balance. Between her and Guy, they got the sodden, limp body of Jack out of the water and laid him on the bank.

'Do something Guy!' shrieked Joanna. He was already pulling Jack's mouth open and blowing inside. He pummelled Jack's chest. Water poured out of his mouth. Then he felt for a pulse.

'It's too late Joanna, he's dead.'

Joanna sank to her knees and felt Jill push her head under her arm. They were both frozen.

'Joanna, we can't stay here, help me carry him.'

They made their way back to the house in silence. In the light, they laid Jack on the scullery floor and saw he had a piece of branch caught in his harness.

'The idiot, he must have been trying to pull the tree out of the water. This is your fault Guy. You should have kept the dogs in if you knew the water was high. You're the great almighty dog trainer and you didn't think of the safety of your charges,' Joanna's voice was rising. 'Anyone with any common sense would know that. Why didn't you do something?' She ended on a scream. He stood there in silence letting her rant.

'Have you quite finished now?' he said with barely contained anger. 'The water has risen in the last hour when we went past earlier it wasn't high.'

Joanna was beyond reason, 'It's still your responsibility! It's your fault!' She began to try and pick up the lifeless body, but it bent and she couldn't get a grip. She sank to the floor and began to sob. Jill came and shoved her nose under her arm again and began to sniff her brother. They stroked and sniffed together. That had Joanna even worse. Guy stood there hopelessly, his fists clenched. He turned suddenly and returned with a large brandy for Joanna.

'Take this,' he said in a stern voice and Joanna did. 'Now get up.'

She did. Then he took her in his arms and held her as she sobbed herself into silence. Finally, she wiped her face on her arm.

'I'm sorry Guy, please forgive me. You could have lost your life in the river, thank you.'

He still didn't let her go. He rested his head on hers. Joanna felt something draining from her. It wasn't the sadness. It wasn't the anger. It was the loneliness. She felt safe. No one had ever held her so strongly. She had never felt so connected with another human being. Then he released her. She was adrift again.

'What do you want to do with him?

Joanna wiped her nose again. She was so calm, so calm as if she no longer had any emotions. She was distanced from the whole situation.

'We have a dogs' graveyard at the back of the house in the wood. We'll bury him there tomorrow. I'll need some help, could you?' Joanna felt stiffly formal. Guy seemed to stiffen up too.

'Of course. Would you like to leave him here tonight?'

Joanna looked at Jill who was still nosing and pawing the body.

'I don't know, she may whine the whole night without him, but it's only putting off the inevitable. No, really, could I leave him here?'

'No problem.'

'We'll bury him first thing. Can you come early with a shovel? I have his favourite blanket I want him wrapped in.'

Unable to say any more, Joanna left, Jill unwillingly following on the lead. When they got home, they both didn't know what to do, so they went to bed with chocolate. But Jill wouldn't even touch a tiny bit of the normally forbidden treat. She was restless and got off the bed to wander around the house until eventually she took herself onto Jack's corner of the sofa and lay down.

Joanna let her be and lay cold in bed, still switched off emotionally, deep in thought. All she could see was the wet hanging head as Guy carried Jack up the path. She couldn't sleep or anything, she didn't want wine, she tossed and turned, went down and made coffee, had a bath at midnight, then watched idiocy on the internet. Dawn couldn't come too soon as she watched the light through the window brighten and at last she could get up.

Jill was still pacing about, looking for Jack and it broke her heart. Finally, she took her for a walk up the garden to the graveyard to see where the hole would be dug. It was filled with little iron crosses with the dogs' names and dates going back to the early Eighteen hundreds. There was still room for more by the iron railings. The place had always had a sad air for Joanna, more than a normal graveyard. Was it that pets had been loved more than people? They made their way back to the house and sat silently waiting for Guy, Jack's blanket over Joanna's arm.

When he arrived, he also had little to say, and they followed his car up to the graveyard. He swiftly dug a hole and they wrapped Jack in the blanket. Jill watched the whole time and they came to sniff him as if in one last time. He was now dry and looked just asleep. They placed him lovingly into the hole and gently covered him over. As Guy patted the last bit down, Jill came closer to the grave and sat. She then lifted her head and howled. A deep sad lament for her brother. Joanna couldn't take much more when Jill had finished, she clipped on the lead and pulled her away.

'Thank you, Guy,' was all she could say, he lifted his hands as if to comfort her, but let them drop. He got into his car and drove away.

Joanna went home and spent the next couple of days pretty well in the same way. Jill wouldn't eat and paced and paced around. She was getting visibly thinner. Joanna didn't call anyone or want company. It was like she had slipped into a pit. When Mia had died, she had never so grieved. And this was only a dog! Maybe it was all the other turmoil making her worse she surmised and picked up another book, only to throw it down after a few sentences.

Saturday morning was just as bad. She was pushing toast around a plate when she heard Guy's truck pull up. He didn't knock but came straight in.

'I've got something for you, and don't argue. I've rarely seen a dog react as Jill did. I think I've got something to help.'

He turned, and Joanna saw to her surprise a large, short-coated but moth-eaten brown dog, with odd ears. When she looked closely, she saw they had been torn and were freshly healed.

'This is Tim. He has been abused, as you can see from her ears. He's quite unaware of it and needs a new home. He was at the Rescue centre.'

He let the lead go and Tim bounced in to greet Joanna, all over her in licks and tail wags. Then a snarl rose from the corner and a black tornado shot out from the basket, growling and snapping at the intruder. Who naturally backed off in surprise. Jill continued to snarl and bite in the air until Tim was well back. Then she stopped and sniffed. She slowly came forward to Tim who sat, tail wagging. Again, Jill sniffed the ears and all around Tim. He sat motionlessly. Then she began to gently wash his ears. Tim groaned and lay down, letting Jill continue.

'Thank you, Guy, oh heavens, that's amazing!' Joanna sank to her chair. The two dogs were now getting down to the usual dog greetings and introductions.

'I don't know how to thank you.'

'That's all right, it happened at my place, so I felt I must do something,' he said gruffly. 'I've got an appointment, so I must dash, call me this evening and tell me how it's all going.' Abruptly he left, leaving Joanna feeling like she had yet another loss to deal with. All she had wanted was his arms around her, to feel the safety of him again. She had to snap out of the limbo. Two dogs again, and a hairy one at that...time for a dog walk. Tim obviously knew about walks and proceeded, to leap about the place at the sight of the couple, then he towed Joanna and Jill down the lane. It seemed like it would be back to Guy for more lessons, and that might be good. Joanna burst out laughing when Jill turned around and looked her in the eye as if to say, what a nutter. Joanna's spirits were lifting. Healing could be so rapid, even if a little of her kept on thinking of the little corner in the dogs' graveyard.

# TWENTY

'Are you busy this morning?' Joanna saw blearily that it was Chloe on the line and the beginning of a week she was dreading. Could they get to the wedding without any major arguments or problems? She sat up in bed and saw it was only 8:30.

'Why so early Chloe?'

'I just thought you might like to come to the house church I was telling you about. Everything's going to go to pot this evening when the happy pair return.'

Joanna thought for a second and that thought contained the idea that Guy might be there, maybe he would be friendlier in church? They had chatted on the phone, but he had been uncommunicative even to her gushing tales of Tim and Jill. She still missed and needed that embrace; wanting to feel it again.

'I'm up for it, but how long will we be away because of the dogs?'

'A couple of hours at the most if we don't linger. Can you be ready by 9.30?'

'If I only give the dogs a quick walk. I take it you'll pick me up?' she said nudging the sprawling creatures on the bed.

'Be ready!' Chloe was gone.

Joanna had been watching the dogs for the past 24 hours. It hadn't all been plain sailing, sometimes Tim overstepped the mark and Jill would growl and attack especially if he was near Jack's side of the sofa. She would take the risk but would'nt tell Chloe a thing. She had yet to tell anyone about Jack and sort of wanted to keep it as a secret, so the pain stayed inside. She left the dogs with the freedom of the house; there wasn't time to see if Tim would cope with being shut in. She was surprised at how nervous she felt as they drove. Chloe filled the time with chat about her lovely new cottage and her moving plans. Joanna began to feel a growing sense of normality return.

'You know Chloe, it's a shame you're going, I'll miss you. You've been a bit of a rock for me lately. There's so much change in the air, and the wedding feels like the most enormous hurdle to get over, as if it will sort a lot of things, which sounds daft I know.'

Then Joanna told her about the business plan and the wanting to find out more of the house history and how it needed doing up. No dog stuff.

'Sounds like Guy has been inspiring you a bit!'

'All we have talked about makes me think I want to study looking after documents and history, but with the show and everything it all seems too much.' Joanna dodged the personal, 'Guy said you found him the cottage.'

'Yeah, he was at a bit of a low point.'

'Tell!' Joanna was doing her best to be upbeat.

'Quite simple, he lost his job at a big kennel where he had trained when they shut down. It had accommodation, so he had nowhere to go. The network in the church found him somewhere temporary until I heard of him. I knew there were empty places on the estate so asked Ray, and we got him the lease. I think what the worst was that his dog he had trained couldn't go with him into the temporary place. He had to leave it with a friend and it got run over.'

'Good grief, he's never said.' Maybe that was why he had closed down after Jack.

'I think he plays his cards close.'

'What also makes me sad is that all this was organised and Dad said nothing. What I thought was a happy relationship seems to have been working on non-information. I so need to sort things with him, we've been going wrong for years.'

'Well, at least my disaster daughter has brought everything out!'

Joanna felt quite nervous as they entered the small house on the council estate, but the greetings she received were wonderful. The small group of six people either smiled or shook her hand then asked her all about herself. There seemed none of the high-tech stuff that Ethan had. There was no sign of Guy, yet somehow, she felt that she wanted this for herself and didn't want the distraction of his presence after all. She was wrong about the technology. They all settled down on comfy chairs and from around her came music from speakers she had missed on the walls. The music was simple and gentle. She could hear little sighs as people around her relaxed and shut their eyes. Then it led into a tune that Joanna knew from somewhere, about being led by quiet waters and safety.

She felt like she was being wrapped in a warm blanket and sat with her eyes shut, relaxing even when the music finished. She blanked out the picture of those deep muddy waters and found this new idea a balm. It was like being held in a mother's arms and at that thought she felt the tears welling up. Not gut-wrenching sobs but an overflowing of emotion that trickled its way out and she just let it flow. She felt a tissue being offered; but it didn't break this soft stream. It almost followed the words that came from the bloke who was speaking,

'We have had a very wet week here and the river Itchen has been high, brown in colour, very smelly with a lot of rubbish in it! How does this relate to a Church service? Well, firstly, our Itchen is the major link that binds our Church groups together. It flows from its source in Cheriton until it leaves the valley and heads to the sea.

'So now comes the religious bit! Jesus is the living water, he walked on it, turned it into wine. If we go to him, are born of water, we will never have to hunger or thirst again. John 7, 37-39. In Psalm 23, the walk by the water is a place of safety with the Lord. Let's look at a typical river.'

As he continued speaking, Joanna's mind filled with images of a pure river springing out of rocks high in the hills. She saw the river widening and growing; flowing with different mixes of minerals and plants. Then the river filling with earth and debris which could be pollution or nutrients to build rich soil. After that, the quiet phase of peace before the sea.

She could feel the metaphor as he talked on about new Christians and their journey to maturity. First full of excitement, active, delighting and sharing to wonder about it all. The spirit of God cleaning and making a new channel. Then the influences of the world and doctrine; polluting and slowing the river down. Then he quoted Psalm 23 again, and the safety by the deep waters.

It all made sense to her; a spiritual, guarding flow of love. Joanna knew she was at the beginning; the water coming out of her was a cleaning process, as she began the journey, from her source into a new land. The pain she had felt at the loss of Mia and even Jack was like the poison of pollution.

Even though the torrent had killed Jack, it wasn't the river that did it, it was the rubbish in it. She remembered how some of her happiest walks were by the river or along the coastline. There was a calming effect in the sounds and rhythm of the flow. It was such a strong metaphor she wanted to sit and think it all through the aspects of her life.

Joanna had hardly given a thought to God in the past few days since Ethan's service. But it seemed something had been working inside her; unacknowledged and unfelt, it was good. All that she had learnt at school and in the local church were river banks that had kept her back from this truth. She was overwhelmed, excited and surprised all at the same time. But she remained in her quietness as the service went on around her. She didn't want this watery caressing to end; she knew it would, and she didn't want to be bereft. She became aware of gentle hands being placed on her and people murmuring around her. Sweet words of love and telling her of forgiveness, and of a love that is unconditional, that would never leave her. A perfect love that would never fail.

'Joanna, open your eyes,' said Chloe.

She took a deep breath and did, and the warmth stayed with her but became a softer, deeper feeling. The tears dried naturally. All the pain of the past weeks was gone. No more tears. She looked around her at the smiling faces, complete strangers who were her best friends.

'Joanna, do you know who Jesus is now and believe in him?'

She nodded.

'Joanna, do you know, and will you acknowledge that things done wrong in your past are forgiven? That you can forgive too. That you can turn away from the bad because you are a new creation?'

It made complete sense.

'Yes, I can. It's like I feel sort of new.'

'Joanna, the old things you will turn away from. But in this life with its pollution of our water, things will come to you and sometimes you will fail. In acknowledging this and turning away, saying oops sorry, do you know you are always forgiven?'

'Really?'

'Yes, really, the love of a perfect parent will show you wrong turns, but will never, never, stop loving you.'

'Joanna, welcome into the fellowship of Jesus Christ. You are a new creation, living in the grace of God!'

At which point the group began to laugh and clap and cheer and try to hug her. Joanna felt like it was Christmas, her Birthday and a surprise party altogether.

She began to laugh and return the embraces. After a while, all calmed down.

'Chloe, did you set me up?'

'Not me Joanna!' She got it.

Coffee, tea and cake were brought in, with the excited chatter going on all around her. It seemed a new language with meanings and nuances that she didn't get but knew she would learn. Another bible was thrust into her hands, then CD's and study guides. She had joined the biggest club on earth and all wanted to welcome her in. As she turned to someone who was behind her, she saw the sitting room door closing. She was sure, so sure, it was Guy leaving the room. Yet it didn't sadden her too much. She had the sudden assurance they would be together again soon. Someone was speaking to her,

'I'm sorry, I was distracted, could you repeat that?'

Joanna found herself invited to a Bible study, a prayer group and a conference until she began to feel overwhelmed.

'Please let me process this a little? We have a big wedding next weekend. I need to read and think?'

'Naturally,' said John, the speaker. 'Just make sure you put a little bit of time away each day when you have some quiet to think and talk to Jesus, to hold on to all of this?'

'Talk?'

'Well, the old school says pray, but that's all it is. Chat to him, and don't hold back. He knows what's going on in your head already.' All smiled and laughed gently.

'Then when you've caught your breath, come and join us again; there's so much more to tell you. You may want to consider being baptised, even though the Spirit seemed to have washed you clean today!'

Joanna smiled but felt a little confused, hadn't she been baptised as a baby?

She felt Chloe's hand on her arm, 'I think we should go. You look like your tank is running on empty.'

They took an extended goodbye, it was almost a wrench to leave the group, but it wasn't the end, just a beginning.

'You may find it all overwhelming in the next few days, 'said Chloe as they drove home. 'It's all so exciting and you're going to want to buzz about while we're all going to be a bit absorbed with the wedding. But when it's over, we'll meet up then I can try and answer any questions. We'll see what you feel about everything. Be assured, you're supported and safe in our prayers. If you want something to do, just read the four gospels. Take some pens, I use colour ones and mark any questions and good bits, and we can look at those. Just keep on chatting to Jesus!'

Chloe was right. Joanna was torn between wanting to run around and tell everyone but also to keep it a secret, hugging it close to herself. She would see how things went.

Finally, she found the courage to talk about Jack, and it didn't hurt like she thought it would. She walked into the house remembering she hadn't put the dogs into their room, but they were simply asleep on the sofa. When they woke, Jill followed Tim's lead and for the first time ever, they picked up a toy each and waltzed around whining and singing in greeting. Joanna felt more loved.

Of course, Chloe was shocked, but she loved Tim, especially when she saw the ears, which in so few days were healing well. Promising to pop in on the morrow, she left. Joanna felt wanted and loved and supported for the first time in years. She bundled the dogs in the car and took them to her favourite walk by the river which now was calm and normal. She felt it a soothing echo of the morning, and she walked by the waters for hours, deep in new, happy thoughts.

Later that evening as Joanna lay on the sofa watching TV, there was a knock at the door. Maybe it was Guy? But outside was Ann with a key in her hand.

'We've poo picked, cleaned tack, all the horses are out, the stables are spotless! All's locked up ready for Diane's return. But I'll be back while she's away on honeymoon. I'm so thrilled she's asked me to step in and run the place. Do you know she even mentioned I might be able to move into the flat! Anyway, must dash, school tomorrow!' She was gone.

Key in hand, Joanna watched the disappearing tail lights of the car. Back to square one. Last to know and least important. This was her house too. If it had to be legal, Mum had left half to her in the will. None of the therapy had made any difference; it was going to be back to isolation in her flat and being ignored again. Diane was clearly still trying to oust her from Ray and her home. Her eye caught her suitcase still in the back hall. Just pack up and go, she wouldn't be missed.

Challenger was grazing in the near paddock, he lifted his head and looked straight at her, ears pricked. Joanna had a choice. She could go on running away like the child she still had within her. Or she could stay and hold her ground; do it in love, not anger. She could take a different path, a new one. She could rest in the love that had found her only that morning. She could handle it in a different way that would make her happy, not bitter. It was a choice.

She was reacting to hearsay, maybe it was just an idea Diane had mooted and Ann had taken as real. Perhaps Diane would tell her, and they would discuss it together. So much would change after the wedding. They needed to set out some parameters and make things clear, so they could all be happy. It could be done. She would have to be a proactive not whining child, and she would keep her house.

Decision made. She was going to stay and sort her life. Maybe staying in one place but doing new things in it was as good as turning your back and running away. She wanted to tell Guy, but it wasn't the time yet. It would come. She was at peace again, the gentle peace that had held her that morning.

Challenger dropped his head and went back to stuffing his face.

# TWENTY-ONE

Nevertheless, such decisions were easy to make in the cool of the evening, facing the reality was something else. The wanderers' late return on Monday morning was heralded by slamming of doors and things being dropped accompanied by loud exclamations. Joanna and the dogs looked at each other, should they escape for a walk before they were found? No, Joanna had made her decision and she would face it. She went determinedly through the baize door into the kitchen. Ray and Diane were having breakfast. Joanna mentally gritted her teeth.

'So, the wanderers return!' she put a big grin on her face, she could do this! Ray got up and engulfed her in a fatherly hug.

'You seem good too, what have you been up to?'

'Oh, this and that!' Go for it, girl.' So how was your time with Ethan and Sue?'

'Brilliant! They sorted us out, hey Diane?'

'They did. I can't believe the things we were doing were so stupid. Are the horses OK?'

'Of course, but you spoke to Ann, she's happy to be coming back, even talking about moving in.' Joanna wasn't cutting Diane any slack.

'That was just an idea in a long conversation, she really is keen, isn't she?'

Joanna relaxed deep inside, her peace had been right. But she wasn't going to stress the subject.

'What's happening this week before the big day?'

'The last fitting of the dress, I ate quite a lot this past week! Then the flowers will be delivered and put in the church, we need to check in with the pub about the food, see if the marquee is ready, then a trial run with my hair, then the rehearsal.'

'No pressure then!' laughed Joanna. It was easy after all.

'Will you come to the rehearsal on Friday?'

'If you'd like me to.'

'Even more, sorted!' Diane grinned.

'No one asks what a feverish week the groom's got.'

They turned and looked at Ray.

'I don't think I need my hair done!' he rubbed his already cropped hair. 'Joanna, you and I need to talk, even before we go to the office. No dog buying, no arguing, can you be ready in an hour?'

'Yes, but first I have to tell you about Jack and introduce you to Tim.'

They both followed Joanna through the baize door and she told them the tale. Ray was all over Tim who greeted them like old friends, and then he made a point of cuddling Jill. Diane stood still aloof.

'I have to go, I'm sorry about Jack but I must go.' Chloe arrived and popped her head around the door and muttered, 'shoes.' at Diane. She just looked at Joanna who smiled and nodded. She was okay. For the first time in ages. They were gone. Ray and Joanna exchanged a real smile.

'It's all right, she's just stressing about her big day. Shall we go out with the dogs after all?' Joanna wasn't so sure about Diane but at last, she was having her quality time with Ray.

'Couldn't we have this chat at home Dad?'

'No, I want somewhere divorced from everything and where we won't be interrupted. We're going to Thorn's Beach.'

They didn't start the talk en route. Joanna couldn't even begin to muster her thoughts. She would have to let

Ray take a fatherly lead. The beach had been a favourite holiday destination as it wasn't known to many people except locals. In accord, they walked along the seawall to the place they had always picnicked and sat down on the grass. The dogs frolicked about, showing off that they were just the most perfect dogs and the best of new friends.

'I have so much to say to you, I don't know where to start.'

'Maybe with Mum?'

'I think a lot came out in the therapy about how she affected your childhood. How you ran to me for safety when she was cross, or you wanted out, or to escape the horses. But in the year before she died, that was less so wasn't it?'

'I was drawn into the pot hunting and the ever seeking to do better.'

'No, it wasn't that. You had Diane as a new friend and you two related to each other in some odd way despite the age gap.'

'Yeah, we did, didn't we?'

'That friendship is something that should last a lifetime. I think you and Diane still have things to sort out.'

'I know, could we go back to Mum for the moment?'

'Right, when she died, we both grieved hard and drew together. In a deep part of me, I felt I had my daughter at last. But you went on with the horses like she was still there, so I went with it. When you suddenly jacked it all in and walked away, it knocked me for six. I felt maybe you might change your mind which is why I kept Challenger. Diane's disappearance; do you remember how you cried when we found the house empty?'

'No, I guess I blanked it.'

'I decided then, I would put my life on hold until you sorted yourself out. I thought it a great step when you wanted your own wing. But do you know, when you gave up the horses, a light went out in you?'

Joanna looked askance.

'You lost all your drive. You began to drift, you rejected university to stay home and run the Show with me. You have lived a half-life. I encouraged you to do new things with it, even take over the running of it. To a certain extent you came alive, but you weren't the Joanna I could see you could be. The only time you sparked was when we found those documents and we made the archive. Oh, and when you got those blasted dogs in defiance of me.' He laughed.

'But you were so angry.'

'I know, it wasn't until we got home, I realised the change in you. But in a twisted sort of way, I still wanted to control. Sorry. And in the therapy, all the resentment of my life on hold, waiting for you to wake up came burning up and I saw it for what it was.'

'So why have we never spoken of this?'

'Just running along in a rut, I guess, taking the easy option.'

'So why Diane, Dad? Is she just an escape route?'

'That came up in the therapy too. No, she's not. I love her for herself despite the age difference. But I didn't see her problems and what she was subconsciously doing. It's all a Cinderella story isn't it!'

Ray grimaced, 'I let her get away with alienating you. You never kicked back, you ran as you did when you were a kid; but I guess you found nowhere to run to.'

'Yeah, you're right. Dad, the reason I gave up the horses was I was terrified I would continue living my life to fulfil Mum's own thwarted dreams. Only thinking of winning and being the best. I had to walk away. I'm still scared that if I ride again, it'll all re-surface and I'll end up on that treadmill again. It ruins being with horses. I still like them for their company and trust.'

'Challenger saw right through you, didn't he?'

Joanna smiled ruefully.' He still isn't happy with me now!'

'Can you make your peace with Diane?'

'I never needed to Dad. You two were so wound up in each other, you never asked me, you never wanted to know my feelings. If you had just said something, you would have found out how happy I was for you. I never wanted you to be tied to me – although of course this has all maybe been unconscious. For whatever reason, I was pushed away and that I did resent. But going back; I guess over time I just got in a slothful rut. Living each year for the show, running on automatic pilot. I couldn't even get an interest in the boyfriends. It all seemed just like too much hard work, was easier to sit in the pit.'

'We've made a bit of a mess of things, haven't we?'

'Yes and no, I'm not the damaged person Diane is because of losing a parent. I'm not blaming Chloe, but Diane was so close to her dad and so aware of the danger he was in. I think her emotions were out of balance.'

'You're probably right there, but I do love her.'

'I know Dad, and I'm happy for you! What will you do next?'

Ray sat up and looked considerably more cheerful.

'Well, after a week's honeymoon in the Maldives, we're coming back here. We'll sort a few things out about the horses and the show, then we're going backpacking around the world! I always wanted to travel; but you came along so soon after we were married.'

'I know it's all my fault!' Joanna was laughing inside and out.

'Oh, no, does that mean I'm totally in charge of the show?' Her heart was sinking.

'Do you think I would leave that with you after all I've said? No, I'm going to employ Sheila as manager. One of us will have to be around on the show days to okay decisions and so on. We've made so much money over the years, which we haven't spent, we can afford to employ her and more staff. We can be free of it.'

Joanna sat and thought for a minute.

'Wow, that's amazing, I feel as if a weight has lifted from me.'

'I know, I feel that way too.'

'Dad, I need to tell you what's been happening with me.'

So, she told him about the business plan and her desire to study and then she got to the house. Ray hugged her yet again and said he was thrilled.

'Dad why wasn't I told about all the things you've done, like the Estate managers house, and the plans to rent it?'

'You know, I'm ashamed, but at that time I just wanted a project that was mine; something for me. It was a manifestation of my resentment of feeling tied to you and the show I guess.'

Joanna took that on the chin.

'Guy showed me what had been done when I left the dogs with him one day. It turns out he's into the Victorian era.'

'Yes, I know, that was why Chloe recommended him to do it up.'

'Have you always been in contact with her?'

'She wrote to me about five years after the disappearance and we kept in touch.'

'And you didn't tell me?'

'Diane was kicking off at the time. Chloe was under stress. I wanted to protect you from her antics.'

'Diane said she wrote to me; did you hide those from me?'

'Not guilty, maybe the MOD stopped them for some bizarre reason.' He shrugged.

'You knew they were here all along?' asked Joanna accusingly.

'No, not guilty on that one, it was as big a surprise to me when I found you two stuck in the cellar!'

'All right,' Joanna collected herself. 'Seeing Guy's place made me look at the house and see it anew. Then when I showed Guy around, I was horrified how we've neglected it. Dad, the whole place needs an overhaul. I feel I want to stay and do it, then use it for the business too. Oh, I'll tell you about that later…I thought I wanted to up and leave, but doing something new with it, and maybe other places like the mill, also intrigues me.'

'Nothing to do with Guy then? Joanna, you're blushing!'

'No. Dad, there's nothing going on. He's friendly one minute and then blows cold! And there's something else I have to admit. How do I say this, yesterday I went to a service with Chloe and…'

'You don't need to tell me! To have a new belief as a Christian, is great. It all makes sense, and Chloe did hint. You appeared lighter when we got back. I have my own doubts and thoughts on the matter, but if it makes you seem as happy as you did this morning when you came in, I'm all for it.'

'I looked different?'

'I'm your dad, I can see things others miss. You were alive as if your fire was relit! I think it's the icing on the cake for all the changes you've made despite the unhappiness with Diane. I'm delighted and relieved that it's all going to be OK!'

They hugged.

'We'll have to meet with the Bank manager, Accountant and Solicitors. I'll hand my half of the house over to you. Diane and I may travel for a long time, so we'll just need a room with our gear in it and stuff to come home to. You will need to know more about the running of the estate, but Stan can do it in his sleep. It won't be a huge burden.'

'Dad, do you think the solicitor has any more documents about the building of the house with the deeds…?'

# TWENTY-TWO

Friday evening, Joanna sat in the cool church sitting and taking on the atmosphere. She had arrived purposefully early for the rehearsal. She wondered about the generations of prayer and worship, did this affect the very stones and spirit of a building? The week had been quieter for Joanna than expected, much of the rushing around hadn't involved her, although she had been roped into helping with the flowers which she had enjoyed, along with a free hairdo when Diane had been in for her trial run.

It had been fun, but Diane had seemed still preoccupied and wasn't chatty. Maybe it was just nerves. Joanna thought and after this was all over they could bury the hatchet and get on with life. But the time hadn't been wasted.

Guy had rung briefly to say he had, after all, found someone from the class who could come and walk the dogs and give them a break during the day. Then he had abruptly rung off before Joanna could make any conversation. She couldn't make head nor tail of him.

She had chatted a bit with Harry. He was finding some opposition to their plans in the office but felt he had a few allies that could leak him the rejects contact details when he didn't handle them himself. Joanna had also found that she could take an S/NVQ in collections care and management; she just had to find someone qualified to supervise her work. She was on the case with the local college for this. Ray, trying to fill the time as he wasn't buying shoes had been with Joanna to the solicitors. She now had a big bundle of documents sat in the cellar ready for scrutiny. There were more maps, documents and plans and she really hoped Guy would lighten up when he saw them.

The process of changing the ownership of the house would take a while. For the first time, Ray took Joanna to the accountants. Even if the business didn't take off and they found the house was about to fall down, the money was there. Sheila had been bowled over about her promotion and had accepted without reservation. They were just left to sort out her job description and a contract. It seemed that it was just Chloe and Diane who were stressing.

Soon she heard footsteps and the wedding party arrived. Ray had Stan with him as his Best man who was already sweating and pulling at his tie as they came in. Chloe was giving Diane away, and there were no bridesmaids. It would be a simple affair with a few relatives and whoever came from the village. The lack of people came home to Joanna, they really had been living in an unknown isolation. Still, Gloria and some of the gang would be at the reception. The Vicar arrived and called them all to the front. Joanna saw that Diane was looking very pale as she came in, maybe she wasn't eating so she could get in her dress. The Vicar welcomed them and got everyone in their places sending Chloe and Diane to the back. He had them march up a couple of times to get their speed right and then directed them to their places, handing over the imaginary bouquet. It was when he got to the 'who gives this woman away,' that Diane exploded into emotion.

'I can't do it like this. It's not right! I want Dad!'

She turned and fled out of the church. Everyone ran off after her. She hadn't gone far. They found her sobbing hysterically on the monument to her father. Ray tried to lift her, but she flung herself back down again. Chloe, for once looking nervous, took control.

'I think you all need to go. I have something I need to give her that might help. Then maybe we can meet again early tomorrow?' All were still shell-shocked at the violence of her outburst, so they left the two women sitting on the grass by the grave. Joanna turned and saw Chloe hand Diane a large envelope. She put her hand on Ray's arm,

'Anything I can do Dad?'

'No, I think I need a little space.'

'No, you don't mate, we're going down the Pub!' Stan grabbed an un-protesting Ray and they strode out of the lytch gate. Nonplussed, Joanna drove home. What could she do? Oh Lord, stop all this pain and let them be happy, please? Suddenly tired when she got back, she flopped on the sofa with the dogs and put the TV on. She was just getting into a film when she heard the baize door swing. Diane came in, holding bottles under her arms, looking happier than she had for a long time.

'Hey, I need to make friends with you, and I have something you need to read!' She slumped down on the sofa and handed Joanna the envelope she had seen earlier. Then she got up and started to rummage for wine glasses and even greeted the dogs. Intrigued, Joanna said nothing and opened the envelope. The letter was from Diane's dad.

*'My dearest daughter, if you are reading this then the worst has happened. I have asked Chloe to give you this on your wedding day, as I obviously won't be there to give you away. I'm so sorry about this. It will be the most wonderful day of your life and I'm missing it. But on your special day, I will be with you in spirit as you walk down that aisle.*

*I know this is sentimental for an Officer!*

*Whatever you have done in your life, it will have been amazing, you're probably top show jumper or something like that of the year. But whatever, where ever I*

*am, I'm proud of you. I was never able to be around as much as I wanted to see you grow, but the times we had together were so special. I used to hate it that sometimes when I was home, I would doze off while you were around, then you would wake me, you minx and I'd jump out of my skin. Every minute I had with you was precious, and I didn't want to miss a single one.*

*Go on forward into your new life, shame I couldn't vet your choice, haha! But be assured of my love for you, my precious daughter,*

> *All My love*
> *Dad*

Joanna found herself welling up. 'Wow that's incredible,' she sniffed.

'Mum said she's wanted to give it to me lots of times over the years. Oh, I wish she had, but it's too late now.' She handed Joanna a glass. 'I remember waking him. I was scared he was already dead, and that's why I had to wake Ray when I caught him dozing, but maybe no more. I just wanted the assurance of Dad's love for me. When he went it was without a word, just the end of another leave. And I've let all this muck up everything. Chasing around trying to find love. I'm sorry Joanna, I've been a bitch, I tried to get Ray from you and I didn't even realise what was going on, I was scared he would go. We were such good mates and we had such fun. Can you forgive me?'

Joanna knew there was no other answer but of course. With that, they gingerly hugged and then burst out laughing.

'I'm hugging my wicked stepmother before the wedding and she can put me in the cellar!'

'Get ye down Cinderella!'

Then it was like a dam burst and at last, they talked properly about the past years, their loves and misadventures. Joanna felt like they were coming home after a long journey. They were just getting to the end of the second bottle and were giggling about some boy they had both fancied when Chloe and Ray walked in.

'We've been searching everywhere for you!' exclaimed Chloe. 'You might have let me know, you ran away with that letter and I've been worried sick ever since!'

'Everything's fine, Mum, I've got my balance back. My ugly little stepdaughter is my friend again.'

'Ugly stepmother you!' and the two snorted like two teenagers. Joanna saw that Ray was smiling and swaying a bit.

'Does that mean I will be a married man after all?'

And he then slumped to the sofa.

'Not if you're going to turn up drunk as well.' They all laughed, except Chloe who surprisingly looked a bit tight faced.

'Come on Mum, join the party, we didn't bother with Hen and Stag things. I'm sure Joanna has another bottle somewhere.'

Chloe relaxed and smiled and then burst into tears. 'I can't believe it's all OK at last!'

Joanna gave her a glass and a tissue and for the first time all sat together and laughed and chatted, even if a bit randomly, until the early hours of the morning, when they all found a wobbly way to bed.

# TWENTY-THREE

The whole tent roared at Stan's anecdote about the time the prize bull had lifted the table with all the trophies on it. Ray had chased him around the ring trying to pick them up and get the table back then fell into a large cow pat. Even Ray laughed as he hadn't at the time.

Sitting at the top table, Joanna could see so many familiar faces and felt for the first time, part of a much larger community. It had been there all the time, but she hadn't understood it. It was also a time of change, and it was a good one; she felt like she was alive for the first time in her life. Stan's speech was now mercifully over, and he announced that the Bride and Groom would take the first dance, once the band had finished their beer. They took the hint and the floor was cleared.

Ray and Diane didn't do the fashionable thing of lurching into a pre-rehearsed show but just had a quiet old-fashioned smooch. Then the band let rip and people got up onto the dance floor and joined them. Joanna too got up to find Gloria who she had seen at the far end of the tent. En route, she bumped into Guy.

'Well, hello stranger!' she shouted. 'Haven't seen you for ages. Shall we dance?' and she grabbed his hand and lugged him onto the floor, the champagne making her bold. They jigged around until the song finished and Guy made to leave. Their earlier synchronicity was gone.

'Hey, what's the matter?'

'Come and sit outside for a while, it's too hot in here.'

Old chat up line, Joanna thought but followed. The air was refreshingly cooler, and she was glad to get outside, even if it was smokier than inside. Guy made his way to the picnic benches in the back meadow.

'Thanks for getting someone care for the dogs for me. And for the help with Jill and Tim. I'll be off home soon,' was all Joanna could think to say at that moment.

'That's OK…umm, how have you been?'

'Never better, the business is coming together. I'm friends again with the bride and groom, and it seems like I'll be doing some work on the house.' He looked more interested at that. 'AND most of all, I made a commitment as a Christian, which is the icing on the cake!'

'That's wonderful for you,' he said stiffly.

'Guy, what is the problem? I thought when we were going around the house and afterwards at the pub, and when you held me that we had made some sort of connection.' Joanna was surprised again at her boldness.

'Maybe we had, but I know you are just using me to help you with the dogs, and things. You've got all this going on in your life. I don't want to be in the way or just on the periphery of this. I want more than this and I don't see that you are ready or willing to have someone in your life that expects that life to be fully shared.'

Joanna was blown away, but it sort of made sense.

'I never thought of it like that, I've never had a real relationship. Just casual stuff…so you are saying it has to be all or nothing with you?'

'Yes. I have a strong belief in the Christian marriage of two equal partners, where each upholds and respects each other and stay true. I don't think you are ready at the moment.'

'Marriage!' squeaked Joanna. 'Could we not just start with the dating bit?'

He smiled, and Joanna saw how he had changed since she'd first met Mr Security Man. It wasn't the weight loss or the haircut, but there was a strength about him she hadn't seen before and it was hugely attractive. A partner and a refuge in a storm. But he was standing up to leave.

'Think about it,' he said and left.

Joanna spent the rest of the evening dancing, drinking and trying so hard to enjoy herself, but it was so difficult. His words and all they would mean kept on going around and around in her head.

They saw Ray and Diane off in a large hay cart. Joanna left and wandered home in the dark, decision made in her usual quick way. It was all or nothing for her too and it had to be now. She wanted Guy, she wanted a strong man as he now seemed to be everything else she was planning could go out of the window. Suddenly there was nothing more important than this. It was only when she thought of Guy that she had any peace.

The dogs were delighted to see her, and she felt guilty from having left them so long, despite their minder. The dents on the sofa showed they hadn't been pining that much. Joanna made her way to bed and as she sobered up; went around and around in her head all that had happened since the show. Then it came to her, there was one way to see if she was ready.

In the early morning light, she got up and put on her Christmas jodhs and her old boots, feeling it was symbolic. The dogs yawned and stretched, ready to follow her even if it meant breakfast would be late. To her surprise, they both went to the baize door to go out. Maybe they were right she thought, she had to symbolically leave one side of herself. Joanna stood for a moment in the hall, seeing her home as it was and as it could be. There was so much good going on in her life, she was finally glad the Diane tornado had arrived, and she smiled. Locking the front door, she and the dogs went out.

Challenger was still in the near paddock, so she climbed over the fence and walked to him. He raised his head and looked as she got closer. His ears stayed pricked as he reached forward and sniffed her outstretched hands. He took a step forward, sniffed her arms, then another step and raised his nose to her face. He snuffed and then put his head close to hers and breathed out deeply. The two stood there in silent communication, which would have been forever if one of the dogs hadn't barked and ran off after a rabbit.

'So, we're good old boy?' Joanna asked gently, and he replied by giving her one of his affectionate shoves that sometimes had knocked her over. 'Come.'

The two walked in peace to the stables where she put him into his old box as if he had never been away. She found what she needed in the tack room and groomed their sadness and mistrust away. She fetched a saddle, for he had always had a spiny back, but didn't bother with a bridle. She led him to the block and got on. It was so familiar and so right. She did the girth and stirrups, and they walked away. For a split second, she corrected her seat and went to get a contact on the mouth. Then she stopped herself. She wouldn't become that mad rider again, it wasn't a fever, she could decide.

It wasn't something stronger than herself and she could see that now. He swung into his long reaching walk and they set off down the lane to Guys. The dogs appeared from nowhere and looked up mystified at what Joanna was doing. But it had to be okay, and they walked beside her in the now misty morning as if they had been horse dogs all their lives. Joanna even had a little trot and canter and it was perfect; rider and horse in perfect symbiosis.

'Thank you,' Joanna breathed and offered this up to him who knew all along. The air was filled with the scent of the newly budded trees and blossom as they wound through the woody lanes. Too soon, they arrived at the cottage. As she was getting off, Guy opened the door, a broad grin on his face.

'That was a quick decision! Are you all moving in?'

'I think this is more symbolic than anything else… Challenger likes me again Guy, I'm sorted.' Joanna stood awaiting his response.

'I can see that, put him in the paddock, it's too early to go down to the Mill to play,' he said carefully. 'We'll all go in. Hello, you rascals!' He leant to stroke the dogs. Joanna let Challenger onto the abundant grass and left the tack on the fence. Guy and the dogs stood waiting at the door.

'No more Mr Security Man,' said Guy, and he gently took Joanna's face in his hands and at last, he kissed her.

## Dear Reader, Thank you!

I hope you have enjoyed Joanna's world and were happy for her. There's another Hazeley book coming soon, 'Compromise'. The sneak preview is after the Thank-yous!
*Please leave a review on Amazon!*
In my blog, 'So where's the Snow?' you can find out more about my books, the background, inspiration and freebies AND my life in Austria!
https://annarashbrook.wordpress.com
You can find my Author page on Facebook and I'm on Twitter: Anna Rashbrook@AnnaRashbrook
I don't do mailing lists, but love to receive your emails, and will send personal updates.  a.rashbrook@aon.at
*Thank you also to my wonderful proof readers, Jenny, Anne, Clare, Tanya and Larry, your input has made this a better book! Thank you to Swingle, my dog, the inspiration for the Barknadoes. Most of all, thanks to Christine Meunier for her help and support!*

God and Dog is a real song and video by Wendy Francis, see it here!
https://www.youtube.com/watch?v=c7ZkSm24xiM


*Now, Dear Reader, please turn the page to read more about the people of Hazeley and enjoy the beginning another story with romance, horses and dogs!*

# Compromise

Mollie opened the back door to let the dogs out into the garden and smelt the new morning. Somewhere a blackbird was singing despite their snufflings and barging about. Dew lay thickly on the grass and the faint smell of the peonies was in the air. Another day, another repetition of lessons, mucking out, cleaning tack, walking dogs. Just where was life going? There seemed to be no direction any more. Both dogs came scurrying in, ready for the next stage of their wonderfully ordered routine which included toast and trying to get the cat's bowl down off the dresser before he had finished. All too soon it was time to go to the yard, and once again the car wouldn't start. Ratty, the black collie cross, sat patiently on the front seat as the flooded petrol leaked away with Mollie absentmindedly stroking her. Once upon a time, she would have prayed about it, but she knew now it wouldn't work. Mutantmutt jealously put her head on Mollie's shoulder, leaving it covered in brown, white and grey hairs. The third turn and the engine chugged sprang into life and they were on their way.

She was still first at the stable-yard, savouring the moment of the twenty eager heads appearing over box doors with low whickers of complete cupboard love in aid of getting their breakfast earlier than expected. The three-sided yard looked like a picture book with the green painted stable doors and red brick. The recent extension had been so carefully done that you wouldn't know they weren't the original Victorian Hazeley stables. Despite their old look, they were one of the best stables in the area, run by Liz of the iron hand, with Mollie as yard manager.

The others always missed this reception as the heads were firmly in mangers when they arrived. Swiftly stepping over the yard dogs, Mollie went to the feed room and collected the premade feed bowls. There was something to be said for an orderly regime. Five minutes in the evening was worth half an hour in the morning, and the new stables had feeders in the doors, so there was no barging in and out of boxes as the horses tried to snatch a quick mouthful. Munching noises filled the yard, and Mollie took the time to look at the horses feeding. All were eating well, no rugs slipped, and hay nets all emptied; that was good. Another routine day; even Keith the stallion was feeding as if he never thought of anything else.

The sound of tyres heralded the arrival of the others – car sharing from the town as usual. Slamming of doors and barking; Mollie's dogs could never get used to the two tschitzus that belonged to Tina. Well, at least this was a job where dogs were welcome. The three girls went straight to the tack room for a brew without looking at the horses, they knew Mollie would have already fed the horses and the kettle was soon on.

'How did the Pub quiz go last night?' Mollie asked.

'We won –YAY!' replied Tina with a smirk.

'Great, I suppose it's the White Horse Inn for the finals then?' Tina nodded, and the conversation foundered. As usual, there wasn't quite enough water for Mollie's coffee, but she was used to it. As usual, she then said, 'I'd better do the feed bowls' and left them to it. Shutting the door, she heard the conversation begin with giggles, and it hurt as much as usual. She looked down and saw she had her purple jodhs on again with the lime green t-shirt. Would she ever learn? At least this time they hadn't laughed and then shaken their heads in disbelief at her fashion sense before saying so. Working alone with Tina or Heather or Sue was no problem, it was just them as a group which made her feel fat and awkward, forever the outsider. Maybe it didn't help them all living in the town and being a generation younger than herself. She should be used to it by now.

Feed bowls rinsed, it was time for mucking out. Mollie went to collect her wheelbarrow; being first, she got the best tools this way. Liz was just coming out of the flat. Maybe today she might get a hack with the kids, and not more lunging…To her surprise, Liz was coming straight in her direction and smiling. Late middle-aged with iron-grey hair, she ran the yard with orderly precision. This Mollie appreciated but not the withholding of information such as the daily ride order. Maybe it was a control thing, yet Liz would never let the daybook out of her locked office. She was still smiling; this was not good at this time of the day. Usually, she went straight to the office and didn't emerge till the yard was being swept, as if there was the most enormous amount of paperwork to be done.

'Morning, Mollie, could you just pop into the office with me?' Mollie felt sick and sicker as Liz twiddled with the locks.

'Do sit down.' Even worse, it must be the sack.

'Now as you know, there's been some conversation about the future of Keith.' Mollie didn't, but this was a better turn than expected.

'Last summer was a nightmare with the mares arriving just as the school hols were starting, let alone with the lack of boxes. So, we've decided to put him free range!' Liz smiled conspiratorially? 'Most of the owners, as you know, left their mares here for three weeks or more, especially when they had to be collected at the weekends. We're going to put Keith up onto the hill, grazing at Chris Brown's place and run the mares with him. He's an experienced stallion man, having had his own stud in the past.'

'What has this to do with me?' thought Mollie, and then the penny began to drop. She was the only one who could drive the box.

'Now we will need someone to go at least once a week with the mares, as most boxes won't get up that steep lane. You'll have to liaise with Chris so that you can do trips loaded both ways. He's happy to remove any shoes, too.' Mollie's heart sank to her boots – all that driving and time away from the yard.

'I'm sorry, this will fall onto your shoulders, but we will try and get Tina's licence sorted out,' Liz was continuing. 'I will pay you for all your time away from the yard as if you were here.'

I should think so, too.

'And overtime if you get held up. You may take the dogs, of course.' Crumbs, getting overtime was like blood and stone usually.

Liz was still smiling, and Mollie realised that for once she hadn't been sure of her reception; she may even have even expected Mollie to refuse. For a moment the opportunity was there, and yet again, with her slow thinking she'd missed the opportunity and it was gone, for Liz was standing as if to usher her out.

'I'm, yes, well fine, but I may need some help unload.'

'Chris will do that; he's met Keith.'

Mollie was grasping at straws. 'What about my regular clients? I'd hate to lose that continuity that we've tried to build up (one of Liz's own mottoes).'

'I'm sure we'll be able to work around that. The other girls can always load and get everything ready, and I'll keep an eye on the book.' Liz patted its closed cover, smiling yet again. 'Oh no, she's lying,' thought Mollie but couldn't see any way to escape or run away from the abyss opening before her. The others would never lift a finger to help her. The one thing that kept her going was that bunch of cheeky kids who came regularly to ride after school. Oh, maybe it wouldn't be so bad; she always reacted negatively to new things. Time away from the yard might be good; the dogs would enjoy the walk if she had to go and catch the mares. If she could just hang onto her

4:30 slot… She gave Liz a small smile and went to muck out.

Six thirty had the dogs investigating the back garden in case there'd been any intruders during the day, while Mollie sat on the back step in the sunshine nursing a beer before she made any decisions about food. All the events of the day were going around and around in her head; she was imposing all the answers and snap humour she should have made. How she had such a struggle with her 3:30 lesson which hadn't gone well until she found out that the kid had been in bed all week with a cold and the mother had pushed her to come. Parents!

Eventually, even Mollie realised it was futile and it was best to put things to bed. She drained her beer and went to see what enticing ready meal she would devour tonight, well at least the dogs would. Blinking as she went into the dark room, she heard the phone ringing in the hall and stumbled over dogs, piles of books and the old carpet in her haste. She got there in time and was regaled with a deeply chocolate male voice asking for her in person. 'If only,' she thought!

'It's James Whitaker, just confirming that I'll be arriving tomorrow morning at about 12 at Rose cottage and I hope all the paperwork has reached you!'

Her heart sank. She'd forgotten the new tenant next door. Why wouldn't her parents just sell the place, not keep going on about keeping it for her to knock through when she needed to expand the house…

'Yes, everything's in order. Your boxes have been put in the garage. I'm right next door, so please just come and knock when you arrive. Are you okay with dogs?'

'Why, are they moving in, too?'

'No, just I have two and they may meet you first!'

'No problem!'

He rang off and Mollie, not for the first time, wondered if she was in the right job. She loved horses but working day in and out with them was robbing her of her joy in them, whereas she could very efficiently organise cleaners and lettings for next door if her parents would just let her. She could make a real going concern with lettings for riders and horsey holidaymakers. Still, tomorrow was the start of her weekend off. She would for a short while be a horse-free zone, and after whatshisname had arrived, she would go shopping. Yes, Primark was calling.

Promptly at midday, the dogs outside began to bark, and Mollie had her hand on the door handle before the bell rang. She'd managed to find some reasonable jeans and a fairly ironed looking t-shirt ready for her trip to the town and was impatient to get going. She had the keys in her hand. What she hadn't expected was the discrepancy between the voice and the person. For what stood on the doorstep was thin enough to be an escapee from Belsen and tall enough to regularly have concussion from the cottage beams. Another charity case of her parents; no doubt reduced rates again. It would be nice to make a decent profit on the cottage one day. All this flashed through her head as she prepared herself to smile. Of course, at this moment Mutantmutt launched herself at her favourite part of the new love of her life, which normally was usually the stomach, but this time was the back of his legs. She propelled James through the front door and onto Mollie, who fell backwards with James landing on her. Momentarily winded and speechless, Mollie could do nothing but stare into a startlingly deep brown pair of eyes. Ratty had come to join in and now was doing her growling at strangers routine with lips bared.

'You did mention dogs, didn't you?' James grimaced and levered himself off. Mollie was still trying to breathe and couldn't answer. He took her hands and hauled her to her feet as she gasped for breath.

'I'm ssooo sorry,' was all she could finally master. 'Ratty, Mutt, basket!' The two knew it was a step too far and sloped off, nobody loved them anymore. James was smiling, smiling too much. Oh boy, she'd really blown it. She was stumped for words and so just gave him the keys.

'I really am sorry, that's never happened before. I'll keep them under control.'

'They don't do that double act every time visitors arrive?'

'No, thank heavens.'

James' good humour was defusing the situation.

'Let me show you around.' Mollie led the way through the gap in the hedge and opened the front door of the adjoining cottage. James followed, and she saw him automatically ducking behind her. Maybe his height wouldn't be such a problem; he was trained. Mollie went into her automatic explanation of the water, heating, bin bags and so on, while James nodded with a pleasant expression on his face and took in what she was saying. Model tenant and landlady stuff, so she was out and shutting the door in ten minutes. Then the embarrassment kicked in, she couldn't get in the car quick enough and escape.

James sat wearily on the sofa and shut his eyes; all that smiling was just too exhausting. What he would have given to have kicked that bleeding dog in the nads, down the garden and onto the road! Still, when you've got a really cheap deal on a let with some peace and quiet to write, what can you do? At that very moment the dogs, now shut in, began to bark. He leapt up and banged on the adjoining wall which, to his relief, worked. Once he had everything set up, he could wear his headphones as he wrote and that would shut the noise out. He saw some of Mollie's jodhs drying on the line and was reminded that was the first time he'd been astride a woman for months, and she was nicely rounded!

He steadily fetched his boxes out of the garage and unpacked. Laptop worked, the internet functioned – you never could be sure in the back of the woods. He found his favourite Cezanne and put that over the fireplace, removing the dark hunting print. In the kitchen, he found no food, just a few tired teabags. A quick trip onto Tesco's website soon sorted that out. He was buggered if he was doing the chatting in the village shop with the locals; he'd done his duty on that for years. Medicines and bath stuff into the small bathroom – no shaving for him for a while. He put his little tin by the laptop ready for later. He slung his clothes into drawers, jamming them shut ignoring the previous ironings. He'd just grabbed a selection when he'd left. The thick quilt on the bed was appealing – a quick snooze, until the goodies arrived, then down to work. He settled himself contentedly under it, not even kicking his shoes off.

'Keith is a completely stupid name for a horse,' thought Chris as the stallion reversed himself out of the box. Especially as he was such a good specimen. A real Welsh Cob, true palomino, quarters to eat your dinner off and a huge firm crest covered by a flowing white mane. No, he wasn't going to think blonde. The horse raised his head and neighed with the imperious voice of his sex, his body quivering with excitement. Tail held like a banner, he then proceeded to try to cavort around the yard. Chris could see it, he was yelling for where the girls were, or if anyone wanted a fight. With an adept yank of the rope, he brought the horse's head down and the rest of him to a halt. He stroked the quivering nose. 'All in good time, mate!'

Chris led him through the stable yard, and out towards the field where he would spend a few nights settling in with his own two mares until the visitors started arriving. Releasing the rope, he expected Keith to take off to his mares who were standing under the tree, completely gobsmacked at the arrival of their Adonis. But no, Keith for some reason was convinced that the action was all in the yard and he paced backwards and forwards by the gate, yelling his head off. His pace picked up and finally, he turned and swung in an arc as if to jump the gate. Chris strode to the gate and waved his arms and yelled, diverting the stallion's attention at the last minute, sending him swerving up the field where he finally saw the mares and the penny dropped. Keith cavorted off to check out the action. Relieved, Chris leant on the gate to make sure all went to order. Mollie joined him at the gate, having swept out the trailer and stowed some bits and pieces.

'Well, I suppose that was par for the course for him. I know he's a splendid Welsh, but I can't help but think he's, well, just a little blonde…' Mollie remarked.

Chris turned to her, surprised. 'Most women are soppy over stallions and their lovely manes! But I suppose when all you can think about is sex, it does stunt the brain cells!' He laughed and they both blushed furiously.

'Coming in for a cup of tea?' he babbled. Darn, he really didn't have time for this…

'That would be great, can I let the dogs out?'

'Sure, I'll let Rex loose; he's not at all aggressive when he's off the chain.' They walked back to the yard and the shaggy old Collie was released to greet some new faces with apparent delight. Mollie followed Chris indoors. She'd known him for a few years through the stables and meeting at shows. It seemed the usually quiet man was more talkative on his home territory. The corridor was lined with hooks laden with old jackets, with hats, boots and boxes on the floor. The kitchen was warm through the aga's glow. It was painted in pale cream with the ever-present huge table littered with paperwork. On the walls hung some tack and rosettes from shows. A home from home, Mollie felt. She could never really do the horsey thing at her cottage because the parents still owned it and kept an eye on her through Jane her cleaner.

Steaming cups in hand, they both sat at the table for a few minutes in silence, both trying to think of what to say.

'I suppose Liz sprung this on you in her usual manner?' Chris finally asked.

Mollie nodded. ' I just hope it doesn't keep me away from the yard too much.'

'I did tell her I could come and collect anytime after hay is done.'

'Yeah, but you'd charge more!'

They smiled, finding their mutual company away from the yard and people suddenly easier than expected, but, nevertheless, they drank their tea swiftly.

'Have you any idea when the first mare's arriving?'

'Your guess is as good as mine; I'm afraid Liz only gives out the minimum of information. I expect she'll ring you the night before.' Mollie glanced at her watch. 'Now I must head back, I need to time these journeys for future trips.' They both went out through the cool dairy this time, Mollie admiring the old equipment that was being used. 'Are you still making cheese then?'

'Just a bit. After Mum and Dad died there just hasn't been the time; I've let things slide a bit. I'll have to get some paid help this summer, I think.'

'There's definitely a market for it here with the increase in holiday people; we have so many more riders now in the summer.'

'Well, I'll see. I just hope that dumb blonde doesn't complicate things too much!' They both laughed and looked up at the paddock where nature was taking its due course. Mollie collected the dogs who were all lying together in the sun and drove away. 'Nice bloke,' she thought. Funny how you never really get to know people when you're always rushing around. Then an image of Chris just now came to mind – he'd been wearing an almost peacock blue pair of dungarees which were too short for him, with an orange spotted t-shirt and the standard farmer's sun hat in green. 'Not just me with no colour sense!'

Printed in Great Britain
by Amazon

51862871R00113